SHANNON BRADLEY-COLLEARY

A NOVEL

HE WRITES, SHE WRITES INC.
LOS ANGELES • DUBLIN • JOHANNESBURG

Originally published in paperback by He Writes, She Writes Inc. 2021

The publisher is not responsible for websites (or their content) that are not owned by the publisher.

ISBN: 9798555573322 (paperback version)

Printed in the United States of America

Praise For The Film

This novel was adapted by Shannon Bradley-Colleary from her screenplay of the *Samuel Goldwyn* film, *To The Stars*, directed by Martha Stephens, starring Kara Hayward (*Moonrise Kingdom*), Liana Liberato (*If I Stay*), Tony Hale (*VEEP*), Malin Akerman (*Billions*), Shea Whigham (*Mission Impossible 7 & 8*), Jordana Spiro (*Ozark*), Madisen Beaty (*Once Upon a Time in Hollywood*) and Adelaide Clemens (*Tommy*).

"*To The Stars* is a beautifully written and stunningly acted film. While it takes place (in 1961) rural Oklahoma, the themes are just as relevant today. It tackles identity, fear, boldness, and regret all through a close-knit population of a small town. (…)

"As women are still often expected to be seen and not heard, this film is an exceptional example of how the tiniest of challenges make the biggest waves. There's a charm about the script and a genuine heart that will resonate with any viewer. *To The Stars* is heavenly."

~ Liz Whittemore, *AWFJ, Alliance of Women Film Journalists*

"A deliberately paced melodrama set in 1960s Oklahoma, *To The Stars* follows the friendship of two girls headed in opposite directions on the two-lane highway of life.

"Directed by Martha Stephens from a script by Shannon Bradley-Colleary, it's a bittersweet story of small-mindedness and self-discovery in a time that may not be all that removed from our own."

~ Kevin Crust, *The Los Angeles Times*

"It's hard out there for Maggie Richmond, the feisty new girl in a sleepy and deeply conservative Oklahoma town of the early 1960s. And under the serviceable direction of Martha Stephens (*Land Ho!*), debuting screenwriter Shannon Bradley-Colleary's coming-of-age drama, *To The Stars*, is refreshingly patient without revealing to the audience why.

"(…) Bradley-Colleary deserves all the credit for leaving the resolution open ended and selling all the possible outcomes to the audience with equal plausibility."

~ Tomris Laffly, *RogerEbert.com*

"Shannon Bradley-Colleary's script and a fine female-centric ensemble (…) make for an insightful and entertaining observation of small town small-minded life. And the unexpected denouement is an unforgettable, impactful twist."

~ Jennifer Merin, *AWFJ*

"The director Martha Stephens, working from a script by Shannon Bradley-Colleary, handles this material smoothly, creating a solid, tangible sense of place with landscapes, gusts of wind and a blue sky that feels more confining than sheltering."

~ Manohla Dargis, *The New York Times*

"The script by Shannon Bradley-Colleary (…) is old-fashioned — which is, perversely, the charm here, right down to (a) simmering (…) subplot that you can sense coming from miles away, like a tornado on the horizon."

~ Leslie Felperin, *The Guardian*

"Written by Shannon Bradley-Colleary (…) there's a grit and urgency to *To The Stars* of something bigger and darker coming along with the changing times."

~ Ryan Lattanzio, *IndieWire*

"The film's keen sense of the barrenness endured by the characters enlarges the poignancy of their loneliness."

~ Edward Porter, *Sunday Times* (UK)

"A stirring coming-of-age story."

~ Jeffrey M. Anderson, *San Francisco Examiner*

"*To The Stars* explores both the stifling restrictions of its time period and of the timeless struggles of adolescence."

~ Cate Marquis, *AWFJ*

"*To The Stars* seems downcast, at first glance, but it serves as a gentle, lovely reminder that one true friendship, even forged amid adversity, can be enough to keep you looking skyward."

~ Mary Sollosi, *Entertainment Weekly*

"*To The Stars* recalls *The Last Picture Show* in its bleak but realistic depiction of how repressive such a time and place was for women.

"High school seniors Iris and Maggie struggle to find their place outside a clique of mean girls. Their limited options are represented by the women around them, from Iris's frustrated, alcoholic mother to quiet, kind Hazel, the trapped owner of the local beauty salon whose plight veers into *The Children's Hour* melodrama but remains heartbreakingly believable."

~ Loren King, *AWFJ*

"Stephens and writer Shannon Bradley-Colleary love their two main characters, so therefore we do, too. And because we love them, we want to see how they navigate their individual and sometimes shared dilemmas (…)

"*To The Stars* presents an authentic, ultimately touching look at friendship – at how two teen girls find something in one another that they need. Iris and Maggie go through good and bad times together.

"The movie brings the chemistry between them alive, showing how having one really close friend during the adolescent years can change your life for the better, forever."

~ Mike McGranaghan, *The Aisle Seat*

"*To The Stars* is a gentle, engaging film well-executed on all fronts."

~ Leslie Combemale, *AWFJ*

Other Books By Shannon Bradley-Colleary

~ *Into The Child: 40 Weeks in The Gestational Wilderness*

~ *Smash, Crash & Burn: Tales From the Edge of Celebrity*

~ *Married Sex: Fact & Fiction*

~ *She Dated the Asshats But Married the Good Guy: How to Go From Toxic Love to Real Love in 12 Exercises*

Articles By Shannon Bradley-Colleary

~ The Fantasy Game That Sparked Up My Sex Life*: The Oprah Magazine*

~ My Name is Tom*: The Huffington Post*

~ 10 Signs You're Dating an Asshat, 5 Tips to Avoid Them*: The Huffington Post*

~ 7 Subtle Warning Signs That Can Help Women Avoid Date Rape*: Your Tango*

~ Remembering Former Love, Brandon Lee, 20 Years After His Death on the Set of "The Crow"*: Medium*

Website

TheWomanFormerlyKnownAsBeautiful.com

Author's Forward

Many moons ago — and I will not say exactly *how* many moons that might be, although the wolf howling at said moons would be long in the fang — I wrote a screenplay in the UCLA MFA Screenwriting Program originally titled *Loving Iris.*

It sat in my computer for four years because it wasn't my husband's cup o' tea. He co-wrote the John Woo-John Travolta-Nicolas Cage blockbuster *FACE/OFF*, so I took his opinion seriously.

(We are still married. He's magnificent. This is his one regret. Well, this and maybe letting me pose online nude — but that's another story.)

Before I recycled my aged computer, I reread the script. Just in case. After so much time away, it was almost like someone else wrote it. I decided the script was brilliant.

This was not to be trusted. I am known to think my own "work" is brilliant. Once, while reading one of my husband's screenplays, ostensibly to give him notes, I laughed out loud.

Turning to me, eyes bright with happy anticipation, my husband asked, "What did you think was so funny?" Scribbling away, I replied, "The note I just gave you."

I sent *Loving Iris* to my literary agent for a reality check. She was effusive. Thus began the journey of a screenplay in search of a film.

That journey had pinnacle moments. Like the year Emma Watson verbally attached herself to star in a movie made from the script, which felt as likely as, say, a kaleidoscopic unicorn arriving to pick me up instead of an Uber.

There were rumors the script was sent to Alfonso Cuaron, Baz Luhrmann and several "hot" Broadway directors for reads. Then. Silence. Ten years of silence. (Fortunately, I was still 26. For the twentieth time).

I had to entertain the possibility *Loving Iris* was doomed to sit on a digital shelf, never to be seen. Unless I adapted it into a novel.

Adapting the screenplay became a journey on par with *The Iliad*. Distractions abounded, like:

~ Raising daughters. Which has many job titles: tutor, chef, chauffeur, comedienne, troubadour, coiffeuse, *Harry Potter* aficionado, secret service, boy repeller and lowly serf, to name a few.

~ Writing run-on sentences in a confessional blog called, *The Woman Formerly Known As Beautiful*. (Which still exists, FYI.)

~ Writing four other books. The best of all, a self-help book titled, *She Dated the Asshats But Married the Good Guy*!

~ Contributing to *O Magazine*, *The Huffington Post*, *Self* and *Your Tango*.

~ Speaking on *The Today Show*, *NPR*, *HuffPo Live* and the lady blog circuit, where I hoped Gwyneth might bestow me with "Yoni egg" swag should we cross paths.

Still, the adaptation process continued spottily, the novel becoming its own animal, with the addition of an opinionated, unexpected narrator and room to dig deeper with character storylines.

Then, just as I was becoming quite pleased with the birth of something new from something I thought would never see the light of day — a miracle!

Loving Iris was claimed by producers Stacy Jorgensen,

Gavin Dorman, Kristin Mann and Laura D. Smith and they wanted to make it. Soon a director, the marvelous, impeccable Martha Stephens, materialized.

Actors stepped forward. Kara Hayward, from one of our family's most beloved films, *Moonrise Kingdom*, and radiant Liana Liberato accepted the leads. Financing came through and we were off to the races.

The team retitled the script *To The Stars* and shot the film in Enid, Oklahoma on a shoestring budget in 2018.

In 2019 the film was selected to be one of thirteen U.S. Narrative Dramatic Features premiering at The Sundance Film Festival.

In July of the same year the film premiered at the Karlovy Vary International Film Festival in the Czech Republic and was invited to dozens more festivals where it garnered acclaim and awards.

In 2020 *To The Stars* was released by *Samuel Goldwyn Films* in the midst of the pandemic, a bright spot for our family in an otherwise bleak year.

Finally, the icing. The Academy of Motion Picture Arts and Sciences Library sent me an email — with the domain ending in Oscars.org (which I will never delete) — requesting a copy of the screenplay for inclusion in the Margaret Herrick Core Collection.

All this excitement thrust me back into writing scripts afresh, but I still felt the gentle nudge to finish this adaptation.

After pouring more time and care into the fraternal twin of Martha's gorgeous film, I believe *To-The-Stars*-the-novel is finished.

It's the story of two teen misfits, Iris Deerborne and Maggie Richmond, living in a tiny Midwest, bible-belt town circa 1961.

They are drawn together by pain and empathy to enter a transformative friendship that unspools in lovely, unexpected and even dangerous ways. I hope you enjoy.

For Ellen, Kathy & Barbara

"To The Stars Through Difficulties"

— Kansas state motto

Prologue

This is not a ghost story. But it is a story told by a ghost.

The year is 1961, but the place — WaKeeney, Kansas — is stuck in the '50s like a June Bug in amber.

WaKeeney's a farming town just north of Wichita with a population of one thousand, two hundred and three. That's damn small if you're a misfit with nowhere to run and nowhere to hide. Which, during my lifetime, I certainly was.

This humble tale opens with a peculiar panorama of the sky at sunrise. That vast blanket of firmament is distorted. Its red-purple early morning hues bleed sharply into the curvature of the earth, as if captured in a prism.

Limited. Enclosed.

This is the view of the sky through a pair of eyeglasses thick enough to suit a noonday owl. The glasses sit on a pile of shucked pajamas and a fuzzy yellow robe at the edge of Sumner Pond, a quiet eddy off the Smoky Hill River just outside WaKeeney.

It's also the place I killed myself.

A dense ring of sixty-foot, diamond-bark ash trees crowd the pond, hiding it from view. A tinge of marmalade on the dark leaves whisper of the coming autumn. The dawning sun sets the pond a-sparkle like a dark jewel.

Except for some Whitetail Skimmers and Blue Dasher dragonflies bouncing along its surface in search of midges and mosquitos, you'd think the pond was deserted.

But then, beneath a shadowy overhang, Iris Deerborne floats into view. She drifts on her back, her hands gently rotating her body with underwater motions.

14

Iris is seventeen. She's a plain girl, with a face as soft as pudding and pale, cornflower-blue eyes that look startled and naked without their glasses.

Thick, black tentacles of hair float around the girl's head like a living creature. Her white nightgown billows out around her ample form in a cloudy embrace.

Iris spends most of her waking hours ashore in our small berg as a hunted animal, which I'll tell you more about later. But here, in these warm waters, Iris is safe.

That's because not *one* of the upstanding citizens of WaKeeney has set foot on the shores of Sumner Pond, much less bathed in its waters, since the suicide-by-drowning of that crackpot she-devil, your narrator, Charlotte Owings.

Small town life can have an incestuous feel, with most folks not knowing where they end and others begin. To WaKeeney-ans, the pond represents my death. And the fear is, if they get too close, it might be catching.

The Voices drove me to my fate. They started whispering after I gave birth to my son, Jeff, and amplified each year that followed.

No one else could hear the Voices. Not my community, such as it was. Not my husband, Ned. Nor the dozen doctors we begged for help.

Just me. Alone with the screaming banshees ricocheting in my head, calling my name over and over, 'til I wished someone would split my noggin open wide so they'd spill out.

On a hot, humid Sunday in June of '51, I decided to drown The Voices in heavy, sinking, dark, dark water and down and down and down.

I still hear voices. Only now they're not inside my broken

brain. They're the thoughts and memories of the still-living in WaKeeney, which makes me a crackerjack teller of this tale.

Iris was no more than seven years old when she first came to the vacated pond alone, but she was quickly becoming a misfit just like me. I often wondered if it was my fault.

Her desperate daddy, who had a wife on the lam from their marriage, dropped Iris into my care when she was newborn.

Though I only had her a year, I worried that as I fed, burped and swaddled Iris, I somehow infected her with my Town Scapegoat germs. That they lay dormant in her child's body right up until I left the post.

When Iris waded into my watery grave, it was like she'd come back to me. Like she'd come home.

I wasn't through with my worldly pain and hers was just ripening. I believe it's unfinished business with Iris Deerborne that's trapped me midway between Hither and The Beyond.

What neither of us knows, is that on this day, the 23rd of September, her life is about to change forever. My hope is, in telling her story, I'll finally be able to move on to a place where all memory of my own story fades away, like a dream upon waking.

Chapter One

"Iris Mabel Deerborne, you ain't endin' up an old maid on my watch! No sir. I'm gonna doll you up, whether you like it or not."

In the Deerborne's humble farm kitchen, Iris peers up from her cereal bowl through a buttress of bangs at the mouthpiece of this edict. Her mother, Francie Deerborne.

Francie stabs a needle into something she's sewing. To say it's a dress is a stretch. The blob gives the impression of an outsized, pink Hostess Snoball confection. She shoots eye-darts at Iris, indicating "the dress."

"This little beauty's gonna help you get a date to the fall prom, young lady."

Between stitches, Francie's perfectly manicured, blood-red fingernails punch a menthol cigarette between her pursed, coral lips. She drags deeply on the butt, exhaling a choking cloud of minty smoke that sets Iris to coughing.

At thirty-three years old, Francie is Iris's opposite. She's brown-eyed and golden-haired. A brittle beauty, like a china doll with fine cracks in the porcelain.

The tobacco soldiers keep her slim and a good bra keeps her shapely. Francie would still be enticing, if not for the acid tongue.

Iris returns to shoveling Frosty O's into her mouth like an assembly-line worker. She's an entirely different person in Francie's presence than afloat in Sumner Pond.

At her mama's kitchen table, Iris is distorted. Like the morning sky through her Coke bottle glasses.

Limited. Enclosed.

Francie's best friend, Edith McCoy, sits across from mother and daughter playing solitaire and chain-smoking, her head wrapped in a bright green kerchief that covers pink rollers as fat as her backside.

Edith's a busybody known around town for being about as discreet as Judas and taking delight in the misfortunes of others. To that end, she privately enjoys watching Francie bat Iris around like a cat with prey.

In Edith's eyes, there's something about Iris that just begs to be squashed, and Francie never lets Edith down on that score. "What if the dress doesn't do the trick?" Edith asks Francie.

Francie smiles savagely. "Then I guess I'll have to sell my body to get that child a date!"

Iris looks up again, mouth agape.

"Sweet Jesus, girl, I'm just pullin' your leg!" Francie laughs. "You got no sense of humor, Iris, none whatsoever!"

"I know, Mama," Iris murmurs, trying to breathe slowly.

I can hear the child's thoughts like she's shouting them down a megaphone.

In through the mouth. Out through the nose. I can't get fretful or IT will happen. And I can't let IT. I can't!

Francie sends Edith a thicker-than-thieves look. "I knew by the time Iris was two years old she had no sense of humor. A real dull spud, and I know where she come by it."

"I swear Francie, you better shut up," Edith smirks. "That Hank's gonna hear you."

"Don't you worry 'bout Hank," she says, taking a long draw off her smoke. "He's out with his cows. His *beloved* cows."

"Still," says Edith, a note of scandal in her voice.

"I told that man, tractors and cattle day in, day out, ain't gonna put much spark to the marriage and now look, no spark to the offspring." Francie jabs a hostile elbow in Iris's direction. "If I hadn't given birth to Iris, I swear I wouldn't know she was mine."

"At least she ain't pregnant like Maddie Forsythe's Jenny," Edith offers, glancing at Iris, "Are you, honey?"

The question strikes Iris dumb.

"No chance of that," Francie sighs. "There's not a boy south of Hays that'd touch her. Here, Iris."

Francie shakes out the dress. It's worse than I first thought. Embellished with swaths of itchy lace built on sheaths of stiff pink taffeta. The construction could stand up and lumber off on its own.

"This is the perfect little prom dress," Francie announces brightly to Iris. "I left a bit of material out around the bust. You finally got something up there, you might as well show it off."

"Mama!" Mortified, Iris crosses her arms over her chest.

"Good God, Iris, don't be such a prude!" Francie turns to Edith. "I sure do wish your Hattie'd take Iris into her crowd."

"I know honey, but I can't control who that girl likes any more than I can control the tides."

"So you say," Francie pouts. She thrusts the dress at Iris. "Now, go upstairs and try it on!"

Just then the kitchen door swings wide and Hank Deerborne shuffles in, kicking mud off his boots. He's a big man. "Gone to fat," Francie likes to say. But under the weight, Hank's powerful, with the muscle from his high school pigskin days still intact.

Many a WaKeeney housewife thinks Hank is plenty handsome, but Francie's knocked the stuffing out of him over the years, leaving the impression of a paper man.

He's brought up short by the sight of the abominable prom dress and shoots Francie a stern look before turning gentle eyes on Iris.

"Ain't you runnin' late for school, Bird?"

"Yes, Daddy," Iris's voice reveals a gratitude that chafes at Francie.

"Well, get goin'," Hank makes for the coffee pot on the stove.

Iris doesn't need to be told twice. She bolts up, hurries to gather her books and in the process, tips over her glass of juice.

"Watch what you're doin', Fumble Fingers," Francie growls, smashing her cigarette out.

"Sorry, Mama." Iris quickly rights the glass, blots the juice up with her napkin and makes tracks.

But before she's out the door, Francie slips the last word in like a knife between the ribs. "Remember to take a change of clean clothes, Iris."

The girl pretends not to hear but blushes scarlet as the screen door swings shut behind her.

Hank stands at the stove, the coffee pot suspended over his mug. Thinking a long, solemn moment, there's really only one way for Hank to sum things up. "You're a horse's ass, Francine."

Once Hank's left with his brew, Francie turns to Edith and whispers, "Well, he oughta know. He's seen enough of 'em."

Edith cackles. "Gal, you are too much. You are just *too* damned much!"

~ ~ ~ ~ ~

Outside, Iris darts across the farmyard, putting distance between the house and herself lickety-split. But as she nears the barn, her pace slows. A steady *thunk-thunk-thunk* means someone's splitting wood inside.

Iris glances back at the house to make sure no one is watching, then sidles up to a barn window, quiet as midnight snow. Heart jack-hammering in her chest, Iris sucks in her breath and peeks inside.

My son Jeff, the Deerborne's hired hand, has his back to Iris, bringing axe to wood.

At seventeen, my boy already looks like a man. He's broad-shouldered, skyscraper tall and as strong as Eulala Benedict's ox, Mamie. But two or three of Jeff's stubborn black cowlicks fight to break free of their Brylcreem slather just like they did when he was five.

The fact Jeff is growing up without me is a torment, even here in my limbo.

He's setting up another log to split when he feels eyes on him. Swiveling, he catches Iris peering in.

She gasps and jerks away from the window like a felon caught mid-crime then presses her body flat against the outside of the barn, making herself small, small, small.

On the count of three, Iris forces herself to move. Panting and stumbling, she freight-trains it for the open road.

Inside the barn, Jeff looks at the empty window where Iris's face had been. He knows she's been watching him since he started working on the farm this summer. He wonders if she knows he once watched her, too? He hopes not, because it might ruin everything.

Jeff shakes off these ruminations and gets back to work.

~ ~ ~ ~ ~

Under the hot yellow morning sun, Iris already drips sweat as she plods along the dirt shoulder of Old Junction Road. It's a straight shot from the Deerborne farm to WaKeeney High School, home of the Panthers.

WaKeeney's having its steamiest September on record, with temperatures rising well over one hundred degrees come noon and lingering in the low nineties all night.

Fresh-cut wheat fields bake flat to the limitless horizon. They're the same fields that haunt Iris's dreams, where she runs from some nameless, shadowy danger.

But no matter how far or fast Iris runs, she always ends up in the same barren fields, like a hamster on the wheel of the world.

Iris is tall for a girl — two inches shy of six feet — but she slumps to hide the height and big bones she inherited from her daddy.

She crushes her books against her breasts, which practically sprouted overnight, and covers the rest of her body under a bulky sweater and long skirt.

It's not just the heat and her itchy sweater that are making Iris flush. This is the second time in a week Jeff's caught her sneaking a peek his way. He knows about Iris's Terrible Shame. The IT she fears each waking day. *Everyone* in WaKeeney knows about IT.

Iris thinks if Jeff didn't find her disgusting before, he surely does now, since he's caught her mooning over him.

22

Neither of them remember the months they lay curled together in one crib under my roof. But I believe that closeness and its loss lives in the memory of their animal bodies.

I wish I could tell Iris that my boy would never find her disgusting. But right now, Iris has other things to worry about. Namely, the '55 Ford pickup that's roaring up Old Junction Road behind her, kicking up a comet of dust.

Iris stiffens. Boys in trucks equal trouble. As the vehicle gains, she caves in on herself, like a gutless jack o' lantern.

The truck's radio blares Ferlin Huskey's honky-tonk tune, "Gone."

> *"Since you been gone — the moon, the sun, the stars in the sky, know the reason why I cry. Love divine once was mine, now you've gone."*

Iris keeps her head down as the truck flies past. She doesn't dare look up for fear the occupants will notice her. Just when Iris thinks she's in the clear, the truck squeals to a stop in the distance, idling.

Iris chances a glimpse. *No no no!* She prays to the heavens. *Let me disappear, let me disappear, let me disappear!*

The driver throws the gear in reverse, backing up until the truck is alongside Iris, pacing her. The devil himself, Mike Whitaker, is at the wheel, running a grimy hand through his forked widow's peak.

His younger brother, Derry — "the Runt," Mike calls him — is crammed in the center of the bench seat. He's a pale photo-copy of Mike and half his size. Hal Beacham, Mike's henchman, rides shotgun. The three boys eye Iris like hounds on a crippled duck.

Mike's the ringleader, the one who dropped out of high

school three years ago because the only kind of "literature" he liked was the blue magazines he kept hidden under his bed.

Mike figured the Navy would take him. He'd travel the world on one of those big aircraft carriers, scoring plenty of "snatch" from the ladies who fall straight on their backs for men in uniform.

But when the Navy docs found a benign, inoperable tumor on Mike's throat, he slunk back to WaKeeney and the bloody boredom of working as a meat packer with his dad and uncles. It doesn't matter how many showers Mike takes, he can always smell the marrow and bone stink coming off of him.

Derry-the-Runt is still a senior at WaKeeney High. But he ditches most days. At home, he gets blind drunk on Thunderbird and dances Zydeco with the couples he watches on *American Bandstand*.

He even sent a letter to Dick Clark, talking up his dance moves, asking to be on the show. Derry thinks he can move just as good as ole' swivel-hips Elvis. But so far, Mr. Clark hasn't responded.

Hal Beacham is a short, snub-nosed towhead whose freckles make him look like a toddler in a man's body. Nevertheless, the Army's taking him, so Hal's killing time in this "dirt-clod pisshole" til he ships out.

That's why he grins with bared teeth as he watches that "stinking sow," Iris Deerborne, scuttle away with her big man's feet tripping all over themselves. *This is gonna be fun.*

"Well, if it ain't old Stinky Drawers," Hal hollers. "What'cha doin' Stinky, leavin' a trail?"

Hal's satisfied to see Iris stumble on a rock, her left ankle folding. She barely manages to save herself from a humiliating fall.

"She don't smell so bad when she's got a pair of jugs the size a melons," Derry says.

On his own, Derry would never say something so crude to Iris. Truth is, he feels bad for her. But in front of Mike and Hal, it doesn't pay to be soft. It's often the weakest folks who act meanest to survive the airless, uncharitable towns scattered across the Bible Belt.

"Them melons're as big as m' Daddy's melons that won the Hays Fair," hoots Hal.

Mike, who's only watched till now, gets an idea. He's quieter than Hal, but far more vicious. "Hey Derry," he says. "Take the wheel."

"What're you doin'?" Derry asks, hoping Mike didn't catch the tremor in his voice.

"What d'you care, just take the goddamned wheel!"

Mike opens the driver's door and hops out as the truck crawls forward. Derry slides behind the wheel, a bad feeling in his gut as he watches Mike jog around the back of the truck, coming up behind Iris.

"Hey Iris," Mike croons, "Can I walk you to school?"

"N … no, thank you," she whispers.

"C'mon Iris, lemme walk ya."

"Grab her tits, Mikey," Hal shouts from the passenger seat.

"Fellas, come on," Derry says, "Leave her be."

"What're you, scared, Derry the Fairy?" barks Hal. "Just do your job and drive!"

Mike trots up in front of Iris and turns to face her, walking backwards, slowing her down. He reaches toward her. "Here Iris, lemme carry your books."

Mike wraps his hands around the books she's clutched to her chest like a shield. "C'mon, Iris, don't be so stingy!"

"Do it, Mikey!" Hal taunts.

"If you lemme carry your books, I might take you to the fall prom," Mike sing-songs, tugging. "You'd like that, wouldn't you, Iris? You'd like me to take you to the prom."

"Please … just leave me alone," Iris begs, folding over on herself.

Mike tugs harder. "Lemme hold 'em, Iris! What're you waitin' for, your weddin' day?"

"She's gonna be waitin' a long time then," laughs Hal.

"Give 'em!" Mike snarls, yanking the books from Iris's arms, slinging them on the ground at her feet.

Iris freezes, panting. Awkwardly, she kneels in the dirt to gather her books.

"She's in the right position now, Mikey!" whoops Hal.

Mike circles Iris, like a hunter poised for the kill. Just as he leans down to grab her …

Thwack! Mike's hit dead-center in the forehead by a middle-sized rock launched at maximum speed. It draws blood and a small knot instantly pops up on Mike's head. "Jesus H. Christ!" he roars.

"Back off, you inbred, bohunk, son-of-a-bitch!"

The three boys and Iris turn as one to behold a girl; a tall, blond Valkyrie standing beside an idling '59 Packard that's pulled up ahead of them. The foursome were so caught up in their own drama they hardly noticed.

But Mike's pretty damn sure the rock that just split his skull came from a small mound of rocks at the intruder's feet.

And the girl is obviously not from these parts. She wears an upmarket, striped jumpsuit that probably cost more than all the clothes the others own. However, it's a perfect outfit for rock throwing.

"Who the hell're you?" Mike shouts at the intruder, carefully testing the bloody lump that stands like an infantryman at salute on his forehead.

"Name's Maggie Richmond," the girls says, like a regular how-d'ya-do. "I'm new in town but known for my excellent throwing arm back where I come from."

Maggie Richmond is Iris's age and just as tall, but lanky like a young colt.

She tosses back her long, stick-straight hair, gold as bullion, and shades eyes that are so dark Mike can't see her pupils or interpret what she might be thinking. Her face is sharp and angular, framed by thick, strong brows arching away from one another like the wings of a hawk.

She bends down and picks up a sharp stone from her rockpile, tossing it from hand to hand, waiting.

"Are you goddamned crazy?" Mike yells at Maggie. "You better get the hell outta here!"

She grins. "And you better turn around and get back in that beat-up piece of shit you call a truck 'fore I let loose on you, farm boy!"

"I'm gonna say it just one more time," Mike threatens. "Hop in your damned car and make for the state line!"

He doesn't like the way the end of his sentence sounded like a question. And why is his Johnson shrinking like a turtle in its shell?

"Come over here and stand behind me," Maggie instructs

Iris.

Mike's face darkens. He can't believe the stranger's gall, interfering with Iris, who's been his personal punching bag since primary school. Why, he'd even made Iris forage for the switches he'd use to beat her. "Don't you move, Iris," Mike threatens.

Iris stands still as Lot's wife. A pillar of salt.

Mike eyes the distance between him and Maggie, plotting the best way to charge her.

"Come over here," Maggie coaxes Iris, as if the slow, quiet girl was a feral thing.

"Don't you move a goddamned muscle, Iris Deerborne!" Mike bellows.

But Iris has gone vacant. She hovers above her body, watching the scene as if it's happening to someone else.

"If he touches you …" Maggie grits out between clenched teeth, "he'll be singing soprano in the church choir."

It's Mike's grasping claw, catching the elbow of Iris's thick, woolen sweater, that sucks her back into her body. Suddenly alive, she launches herself, like one of those heat-seeking missiles, to duck behind the striking inferno of a girl.

"Mike, what're you doin'?" shouts Hal, spittle flying off his lips.

"What're *you* doin', chicken shit?" Mike bawls. "You're the goddamned grunt. Whyn't you come on out?"

Hal stays put. "Where you think you're goin', Iris?" he asks, hoping to put Mike's attention back where it belongs.

"You better get over here right now, Stinky," Mike snarls.

But Iris maintains her position behind Maggie, head

down. Waiting.

Mike's pride can take no more of this disrespect. The blonde bitch's eyes crackle with rage, so Mike focuses on her narrow waist.

He crouches, ready to slam-grab her in the same tackle that won the WaKeeney Panthers the regional championship.

Mike charges. *Whack!* Another stone impales his chest near his heart. He wonders if this is what it feels like to be shot at point-blank range. "Jesus H. Christ!" he cries, "You do that one more time and you'll be sorry!"

"Will I be sorry 'cuz I forgot my manners or 'cuz you're gonna *do* something about it?" Maggie taunts.

Her black snake eyes make the hairs rise on the back of Mike's neck. He shoots a look at Derry and Hal. Derry's a soft bastard, but Mike can't lose face in front of Hal. He rushes Maggie like he's coming off the line, all head and shoulders.

Crack! Smash! Bash! Smack!

The first rock splits the top of Mike's head. The second draws blood from his ear. The third slices into his shoulder. The fourth near-breaks his nose.

"I said move it, move it, move it!" Maggie shouts, firing away. She's not backing up but lunging forward with each rock torpedo.

Mike's got his hands up, protecting his head. He's like the Titanic trying to come about on a too-small rudder. When he finally turns his back in a self-protective hunch, Maggie starts in on the truck.

Hal furiously rolls up the passenger window as a rock whizzes past his left ear. *Crack!* A hairline fracture runs down the windshield.

"Come on, Mike! Let's git!" Derry yells from behind the wheel.

That's all Mike needs to hear. He hauls ass. "This ain't over, bitch!" he shouts.

Maggie gifts Mike another rock in the back of the head for that. As he hops the tailgate, Derry throws the truck in gear and they peel out.

Smash! Maggie knocks out a tail light for good measure. "Cow fuckers!" she hollers at the retreating truck.

Iris stares at Maggie, thunderstruck. Her savior is the most stunning person Iris has ever seen. But when Maggie turns those impenetrable eyes on Iris and asks, "Are you okay?" Iris looks away and swallows hard. She could swear she sees pity. And though Iris thinks she might *be* pitiful, she doesn't want pity.

Without a word, she hurries to her strewn books, hunkers down and gathers them up.

"We gotta turn those bastards in," Maggie exclaims. "Bastards!" she bellows after the truck, still shrinking in the distance.

Iris does an about-face, clutches her book armor, and doggedly sets off for school.

"Hey, where you goin'?" Maggie trails Iris. "You should stop a minute. You're probably in shock or somethin'."

Iris marches on with Maggie keeping pace. "Look, I can drive you, if you want."

Iris's body might still be there, but the rest of her is gone.

"It's my mouth, isn't it?" Maggie asks, regretfully. "I'm sorry, I got a mouth like a gutter." By way of explanation, "I'm from the city."

Iris presses on. Maggie stops in her tracks. At a loss.

What is wrong *with this girl? Is she slow in the head? Or does she just have bad manners?*

"You don't have to thank me," Maggie shouts at Iris's retreating figure, "It's not like I risked my life or anything!"

Maggie watches Iris dwindle away. Finally, she stoops, picks up one last rock and launches it as hard and as far as she can into the endless, dry wheat fields. A puff of dirt marks its crash landing.

"Welcome to Kansas!" Maggie shouts, the sound of her fury swallowed up by the great, wide, empty sky.

Chapter Two

WaKeeney High isn't much to look at. It's a middling, flat-roofed, two-story, red-brick building boasting one hallway of lockers.

It's got a lunch yard dotted with a dozen scattered tables and two dirt parking lots that Principal Shanley says he's going to asphalt every summer, but never does.

The school is populated just enough to support a yearbook staff of two: Susie Short and Angela Johnson, sophomore photographers who consider themselves artists and make several yearbook cameos the way Hitchcock does in his films.

There's also the Dauntless Debate Club that has yet to compete in its five-year tenure. The Quilt-Making Society, which specializes in farm-themed creations. The Songbirds cheer squad, a coven of girls known to eat their own, figuratively speaking.

And finally, the Panthers football team: all first-stringers since there aren't enough boys for subs. If anyone gets injured, they've got to call the game.

With a handful of exceptions, all the students at WaKeeney High have known each other since they were knee-high to a grasshopper and their set-in-stone social roles were decided long ago.

~ ~ ~ ~ ~

When the school bell clangs the start of this particular day, each of these students is in class. All but one.

Like a prairie dog peeking out of its burrow, Iris pokes her head out of the girl's bathroom. She surveys the hallway and, seeing it empty, darts to her locker. Clumsy fingers work the combination lock. Iris fails once, twice, but on the third try the tumbler *clicks* and the lock snaps open.

Panting, Iris reaches into her locker and pulls out a ragged Beckman's Grocers bag with something bundled inside. She eases her locker door closed with a *snick*, then falls back to the girl's bathroom.

Once inside, Iris ducks into a toilet stall and locks the door behind her.

She leans against one wall, taking two big breaths — *in through the mouth, out through the nose* — then places the grocery bag on the floor.

Iris tries to unbutton her skirt but her clenched fingers just don't seem to work.

In a panic, she rips at the buttons. They fly in all directions, bouncing off the toilet stall's metal walls as Iris yanks the skirt off and kicks it away.

Her Terrible Shame has drenched the skirt, turning it a mottled gray. Her under garments, the inside of her thighs, and even her socks are wet, too.

Iris strips urine-soaked drawers from her hips and down her legs. She tugs each sock off. Then claws a foot of toilet paper from the roll, drying herself as best she can. *Breath in through the mouth, out through the nose.*

If only Iris's Terrible Shame could be contained within the four walls of this toilet stall, maybe then … maybe then … but there is no "then" Iris can imagine. She barely remembers the time before she was called Stinky Drawers.

Calmer now, Iris fishes into the paper bag and retrieves a pair of clean underwear and a thick sanitary pad. She carefully pins the pad to the underwear, then pulls it on.

Next, she reaches into the bag and brings out a clean

skirt, numbly stepping into it and buttoning it at the waist.

Like an automaton, Iris fingertips her soiled garments and drops them inside the bag. She folds it down once, twice, three times, until it's locked up safe.

Iris picks the bag up, clasping it to her waist, when suddenly a wave of dizziness strikes. It lands her hard on the toilet seat, the bag in her lap.

Iris's head drops. The glasses fall off her face, landing, unbroken, at her feet. Tears overflow her swollen, sightless eyes.

~ ~ ~ ~ ~

"Alright, class, simmer down, now. I want to introduce you to this lovely young lady, Margot Richmond …"

Miss Steingarten, the squat, wide-as-she-is-tall chemistry teacher, presents Maggie in front of her class as if the girl was a debutante at the Harvest Ball.

Maggie cringes at the sound of her given name. It seems to belong to someone else.

"Maggie," she corrects Miss Steingarten.

"Excuse me, dear?"

"I'm called Maggie."

"Well, that's fine," Miss Steingarten says. "Margot comes to us all the way from Saint Louis, Missouri. I expect you to welcome her to our humble community with Panther pride. Let's show Margot that we may be small, but we have a big heart!"

What Maggie doesn't know is that Clarissa Dell, trend-setter and maven of this scrubby little whistle-stop, has been bathing her in a fiery attention from the second row.

Clarissa's been nothing but a boon to her parents, for

from their mousy, inbred loins sprang perfection. Clarissa was born with blonde ringlets and eyes as aquamarine as the Mediterranean she plans to visit someday.

With her good looks and flirty vivacity, Clarissa has every certainty she'll land the biggest fish in a much bigger pond after graduation.

There's been town speculation, after hot summer barbecues where strong spirits were imbibed, that Iris Deerborne and Clarissa Dell were swapped at birth.

The girls were born on the same day at Saint Crispin's Hospital in Potwin, just an hour and forty minutes apart.

Clarissa seems like a chip right off Francie Deerborne's block. They've both been head cheerleader of the Songbirds and Queen of the Neewollah Festival ("Halloween" spelled backwards).

Just like Francie in her youth, Clarissa worries she bears the stench of Small-Town U.S.A. And she can tell, with barely a glance, that Margot-Richmond-from-St. Louis-Missouri bears no such odor. Clarissa instantly hates her.

"If that's what they wear in the city, you can have it," she stage-whispers to her minion, Rhonda Robertson, a redhead with a highly suggestible nature and an unfortunate platoon of pimples marching across the bridge of her nose.

"She's pretty, though," Rhonda notes.

"In a hard sort of way," Clarissa replies.

"Yes, I can see that." Sweat droplets pop out on Rhonda's upper lip for fear she might've raised Clarissa's dander.

Rhonda is rescued from her blunder when the classroom door ekes open just wide enough to admit Iris. "Iris Deerborne's late again," Rhonda announces, redirecting

Clarissa's attention.

"Iris," Miss Steingarten seems to shout from the rafters, "Why're you tardy this time?"

"I uh … I uh …" For the second moment that day, Iris would love nothing more than to vanish into the ether.

"Speak up, Iris, I can't hear you!"

"I had to go to the nurse's office," she responds weakly.

"I swear, Iris, you're there so often you may as well bring a suitcase and take up residence. I don't suppose you brought a note this time?"

Iris stands mute.

"Oh, never mind," Miss Steingarten sighs. "Just sit down."

Iris sinks gratefully into her chair. She notices Maggie standing at the head of the class. Their eyes meet briefly. Then Iris looks down at her hands.

"Okay, people," Miss Steingarten addresses the room at large. "This week we're breaking minerals down into aqueous solutions. I expect you all to be responsible with your Bunsen burners. Last year Janine Stewart's eyebrows were singed, as you may recall, and the school is liable."

Miss Steingarten grabs a list of names off her desk. "Iris Deerborne, Clarissa Dell, you'll work at station one."

"Can't we switch partners this week, Miss Steingarten?" Clarissa asks.

"I already told you no, Clarissa."

"I don't see why I keep gettin' stuck with Iris just 'cuz we're both D's!" The ask has become a whine.

Students titter. Maggie casts a sharp glance at Clarissa and quickly understands the hierarchy of the classroom.

"We don't have time for social preferences, Clarissa," Miss Steingarten sighs, with the fatigue of a thirty-year high school teaching veteran. "We've got elements to break down and they could care less who your partner is."

~ ~ ~ ~ ~

At station one, Clarissa holds a teaspoon of sulfur over a flaming Bunsen burner as Iris hovers behind her.

"Um, I don't think you're supposed to hold the spoon so close to the flame," Iris tells Clarissa.

"Iris, which one of us currently has a B-minus in chemistry?" Clarissa asks.

Iris sets her chin. She'll be damned if she answers *that* question. She might be the town pariah, but she can be stubborn too.

"I currently have a B-minus in chemistry, Iris," Clarissa answers her own question. "And what do you have?"

Iris keeps mum.

"What. Do. You. Have?" Clarissa demands.

"A C," Iris mutters.

"That's right, a C. And is a B-minus better than a C?"

"It's just … if you hold the sulfur too close to the flame it can catch on fire," Iris persists.

"Just answer the question."

"A B-minus is better," Iris grudgingly admits.

"A B-minus is better. You got that right," Clarissa responds. She looks down at her spoon, wrinkling her nose. "My God, Iris, this burning sulfur smells almost as bad as you do."

Across the table, Maggie works alongside Rhonda. She's caught Clarissa's remarks and looks as if she wished she'd held on to that pile of rocks.

"So, what'd he do?" Clarissa asks, looking directly at Maggie.

"What did who do?" Iris responds, confused.

"I wasn't talking to you, Iris. I was talking to Miss Big-City."

Maggie meets Clarissa's cunning gaze over their beakers. "I'm sorry, I wasn't paying attention. What'd you say?"

"I said, what … did … he … do?" Clarissa enunciates, as if speaking to a soft-brained idiot.

"Who?"

"Your daddy? He musta done somethin' wrong to land y'all in WaKeeney." Clarissa gazes about, seeking an audience. "Did he drink away the family fortune? Was it gambling? Is his criminal rap sheet long as his arm?"

Iris and Rhonda hold their breath, awaiting Maggie's response.

"Is that *your* daddy's story?" Maggie asks sweetly. "You seem to know it so well."

For the first time in she-can't-remember-when, Iris smiles. And Rhonda, Lord help her, giggles.

"What're you laughin' at?" Clarissa spits at Rhonda, who flails like a fish on a dock.

"Nothin' … I was just … nothin'."

Clarissa swivels back to Maggie, "My daddy developed terraced farming. He pretty much single-handedly saved the Great Plains from the Dust Bowl happenin' all over again."

"He's the richest man in the tri-county," Rhonda pipes up.

"Is that right?" Maggie asks.

Clarissa deems Maggie's tone under-impressed. "That's right."

Iris sneaks a peek at the new girl, eager to hear what might come out of her unpredictable mouth next.

The group works in silence, heating their sulfur into a straw-colored liquid, though Clarissa's is turning brownish black.

Maggie breaks the silence. "Well, my daddy never did anything quite so grand as 'single-handedly' saving the Great Plains from another Dust Bowl. He just takes pictures for *Life* magazine."

"He does not!" Clarissa exclaims. Maggie shrugs her indifference. Another stretch of silence descends. But Rhonda and Clarissa exchange dying-to-know-more glances. Iris is dying to know more, too, but busies herself cleaning up the excess sulfur powder on the tabletop.

"If your daddy's some hot-shot photographer," Clarissa prods, "why'd y'all come to WaKeeney?"

"You ever heard of Edward R. Murrow's documentary *Harvest of Shame*?" Maggie asks.

"Of course," Clarissa snorts, as if the answer should be obvious to any fool.

"What was that again?" Rhonda asks Clarissa.

"It's a ... it's a ..."

A small voice interrupts. "It's a documentary about the exploitation of migrant farm workers," Iris says, before calculating the cost of tutoring her tormentor.

"I already knew that Iris, you don't have to tell me!" Clarissa snaps.

"You seemed a little confused." Maggie purrs, meeting Iris's eyes with the barest hint of cahoots.

39

"Well, I wasn't confused," Clarissa flusters.

"Anyway," Maggie continues, "Daddy's been asked to do research on migrant practices in the farm communities. A 'Hardened Heart of the Heartland' sort of thing, capturing local color and all. So, we had to come here."

Maggie warms to her story, polishing it like a crystal. "I didn't wanna move to some podunk, backwater farm town and soon as I graduate, my folks'll see nothin' but my jet fumes, 'cuz I'm gonna be an airline hostess. They already interviewed me in Saint Louis and said I could have a job once I'm nineteen. Then I'll travel the world."

"I've been to Hays!" Rhonda offers.

Clarissa shoots her a *shut-your-yap* look.

"Take my daddy, for instance," Maggie continues. "He flies all over the world for *Life* magazine. You might've even seen the picture he did of Marilyn."

"Marilyn Monroe?" Rhonda squawks.

"Who do you think?" Clarissa barks, her Maggie-approval rating growing perceptibly.

Iris, on the other hand, looks at Maggie cock-eyed. There's something she can't quite put her finger on, something that just feels … off.

"Mostly he does political events. You know, wars, summit meetings, things like that," Maggie continues. "But every now and then they need him in Hollywood to take some famous person's photo. Celebrities are real picky about who shoots 'em. Especially Marilyn 'cuz she's sensitive about her nose. She had rhinoplasty, which most folks don't know."

"We knew that, didn't we Clarissa?" chirps Rhonda as she tests the pertness of her own button nose with a pointer finger.

"Of course we knew. Everybody knows that," Clarissa nods benevolently at Maggie, "You may continue …"

"Well, Daddy understood just how Marilyn'd want her nose to look when he photographed her and he was right on the mark."

Suddenly Iris laughs. It's an abrupt, snorting laugh that line-drives right through Maggie's story. She slaps a hand over her mouth to make it stop.

Chalking this outburst up to just another Iris oddity, Clarissa and Rhonda circle the wagons around Maggie.

"You should be a Songbird," Clarissa announces.

"Oh, my gosh!" exclaims Rhonda. "She'd fit right in with the girls!"

"Mrs. Hibbard loves us," Clarissa says. "We can get you in, no problem."

Iris looks down. She can almost hear the *click* that includes Maggie in a social world she can never enter. Iris is so preoccupied by this disappointing fact that it takes her a second to notice Clarissa's sulfur spoon has burst into flame.

"Jump down Jesus!" Rhonda shrieks, "Clarissa, you're on fire!!"

And indeed, one of Clarissa's blonde ringlets is ablaze. She shrieks like a gut-shot magpie, drops the fiery spoon onto the tabletop and fans her head in a panic, which only feeds the flames.

Across the classroom, Miss Steingarten shouts, "For the love of God, someone put that girl out!"

Splat! Iris dumps a 1000-milliliter beaker of water over the top of Clarissa's head, extinguishing everything but Clarissa's temper.

"Goddamn you, Iris!" she sputters. "You absolutely

41

destroyed my silk peplum blouse! I told you to watch my sulfur spoon!" Clarissa whirls around. "Miss Steingarten! It's Iris's fault. She caught me on fire!"

"Nothing is ever your fault, is it, Miss Dell?" Miss Steingarten grouses. "Well, I'll have you know …"

As Clarissa and Miss Steingarten argue, pandemonium erupts — students laughing and howling, igniting more sulfur, throwing beakers of water at each other.

In the chaos, Iris and Maggie catch each other's eye.

If you were a dust mote floating in the beam of sunlight above Clarissa's charred head — or a ghost invested in the outcome of one particular outcast — you might notice an exchange of energy between the girls that forms itself into discreet, satisfied, shared smiles.

Chapter Three

Iris flinches when she hears the low hum of an engine behind her as she walks that same ribbon of highway home from school.

Adrenaline shoots through her body. She prays her bladder holds when Mike the-devil's-spawn Whitaker confronts her again.

Iris thinks she should've let him feel her up instead of allowing Maggie Richmond to save her carcass. Now Mike won't want to just humiliate her, he'll want to hurt her.

She's been lucky so far, dodging his filthy reach because of his working hours at the meat-packing plant. Now she wonders if he's started working the graveyard shift again, leaving his mornings and afternoons free to torment her.

As the engine hums closer yet, Iris implores an absent God, *Let me disappear. Let me disappear. Let me disappear. Just this once!*

Iris's prayer is answered indirectly when it's Maggie's Packard that pulls even with her.

The new girl leans her head out the open window. "Hey Iris, you wanna ride?"

Relief washes over Iris's face. But she hesitates, sure she sees it again. Pity written all over Maggie Richmond's face.

"That's okay, I like to walk." She turns away as Maggie stares, confounded by Iris's response.

Iris's step is resolute. And so is her thinking about Maggie. I can hear it just as plain as if she shouted.

It's just a matter of time before she finds out why everybody calls you Stinky Drawers and that'll be that. She'll never talk to you again.

43

"I can give you a ride no problem," Maggie persists. "We're goin' the same direction."

"You don't have to make friends with everybody," Iris snaps, startled by her own anger.

"I don't wanna make friends with everybody." The note of sadness in Maggie's voice perplexes Iris.

No matter, Iris thinks as she marches on. *Soon enough she won't like you. Soon enough she'll think you're foul.*

Maggie paces Iris a moment longer until she realizes it's no use. "Suit yourself." Maggie stomps on the gas pedal, leaving spumes of dust in her wake.

Iris can't help watching Maggie's car disappear in the distance, like a chariot bearing Athena.

~ ~ ~ ~ ~

Hazel Atkins's Beauty Salon is a humble operation. It's located in a rinky-dink, detached garage off a tidy Craftsman bungalow with a postage-stamp yard, a patch of fading grass, and a wrap-around porch.

Hazel inherited the house from her Aunt May when the elder passed during a particularly violent flu season a year ago.

May had been a childless widow. Childless thanks to a tilted uterus and malfunctioning ovaries, or so we'd all heard from Dr. Smithlove's receptionist way back when. And widow thanks to her husband's unfortunate run-in with a combine five years earlier.

That left May with only Hazel in her life, which was not particularly satisfactory to either party.

Despite being six towns away, May immediately made clear her disapproval of Hazel's "lifestyle."

As she would point out in a series of increasingly critical

missives, Hazel, at the ripe age of twenty-two, was bereft of husband, child, or even a steady beau. Spinster material!

"I just can't understand why a good-lookin' young gal like yourself — even if you could stand to wear a more supportive brassiere — can't find a nice young man to marry!" May would carp on Hazel's infrequent visits.

Hazel was indeed a "perfectly attractive young woman," as her aunt would say — graced with two charming dimples on either side of her mouth, a dainty upturned nose and thick-lashed eyes the same color as her name. And she'd had her fair share of marriage proposals.

But Hazel told her aunt she was holding out for the "most wonderful" man, and that she'd yet to meet one who'd come close to her deceased Uncle Teddy.

Even May couldn't argue with that kind of logic. What she didn't know was that Hazel had been very much in love once before. But when that love affair crashed and burned, she couldn't bear to risk suffering so badly ever again.

Hazel was surprised at her devastation when her opinionated, bossy aunt died. But grateful when she learned May willed her the small house, because it meant Hazel could move far away from the love-that-could-never-be.

So it's a composed Hazel who's here now, setting curlers, painting nails and glad of it. Then, of all things to happen on a WaKeeney Wednesday, here comes a brand-spanking new, Cadillac LaSalle pulling up to Hazel's own curb, with a hood longer and sleeker than Cyd Charisse's thighs.

And behind the leather-wrapped wheel is none other than Maggie Richmond's mother, Grace, who will soon become a flung stone that casts ripples into Hazel Atkins's life. But I'm getting ahead of myself.

Let's talk a bit more about Grace.

The first thing you should know is that Grace Richmond comes from Old Money. Landed gentry and so forth. And Grace's family had a lot of that generational lucre.

Like a fish that doesn't know it swims in water, Grace has little idea how her unconscious expression of that wealth inflames the rampant envy of Have-Nots.

WaKeeney locals — dyed-in-the-wool Have-Nots — first saw Grace driving her Caddy down Barclay Avenue to Butcher Bens this very morning and had plenty to say about it.

Outside the Dime & Save, Nettie Hornbottom told Julissa Green, "That kinda neighbor's about as popular as a wet dog at a parlor social."

Inside Darnell's Barbershop, Garrison Henry informed Butch Frain, "That cupie doll's gonna last here 'bout as long as a pint of whiskey at a five-handed poker game."

And right by The Church of the Savior Our Lord, Neila Sean grumbled to Honora Johnson, "I didn't know Saint Louey Whoo-ers could drive!"

And that was before any of them got an eyeful of Grace's get-up. Currently, Grace's slender feet, encased in salmon pink Dior pumps, have emerged from the Caddy and are tap-tap-tapping their kitten heels toward Hazel's salon.

Grace's ripe figure is perfectly set off by a chic full-skirted day dress, complemented with matching garnet cap, a pearl and gold brooch in the shape of a Phoenix, and blameless white gloves.

And if her wealth weren't enough to annoy the locals, there's also her beauty to contend with. Grace has her daughter's dark eyes, but where Maggie is slender as a reed, Grace is rich hills of feminine curves. Where Maggie's light-haired, Grace has thick, sleek black hair rolled into a stylish mound the Frogs call a "chignon."

Framed by the parched Kansas panorama, Grace looks like a blush rose that accidentally took root on a dirt-caked highway.

As Grace tiptoes over the cracks in Hazel's driveway, swatting a cloud of no-see-ums away from her face as she goes, you have to wonder what on earth made Grace trade big sidewalks and glass-display windows for this backwater.

Chin up, deep breath, and Grace, who looks visibly nervous, opens the salon door and advances inside. A tinkling bell announces her arrival.

One glance around the room takes in the single hair-washing sink, two manicure/pedicure chairs and one shabby lounger sporting a hairdryer bell on a bendable stem.

Hazel's only customers, Edith McCoy, Francie's early-morning, kitchen-table companion, and Barbara Dell, Clarissa's washed-out, busy-bee mama, gawk as Grace "waltzes in," bedazzling in her finery.

Edith's elephant feet soak in a tub of hot water as Hazel polishes her fingernails. Barbara waits for the vanishing cream on her thin upper lip to remove a light mustache as the permanent curlers in her mousy brown hair do their utmost to transform her into something less ordinary.

"I don't know 'bout you," Edith whispers to Barbara, "but I suddenly feel like a sow at a pony show."

Barbara sniffs, "Not me! What kinda person puts on airs to get their feet buffed?"

Sensing their disapproval, Grace's chin drops and she pulls anxiously at her gloves.

Hazel steps to the rescue. "May I help you?" she asks warmly, as if this kind of vision appeared daily and twice on

47

Sundays.

"Oh, yes, yes, thank you. I'm Grace Richmond? I think I have a two o'clock appointment?"

Hazel leaps up to check her scheduling book. "Yes, Mrs. Richmond, you absolutely *do* have a two o'clock. But you look like you've already been to the beauty parlor."

"Aren't you sweet," Grace murmurs, coloring with relief.

That Hazel. She can take the temperature of a room from a Mississippi mile.

"Here, why don't you change into this." Hazel hands Grace a black smock that opens in the front. "Then I'll get started on your hair right away. You can change over there."

Grace thanks Hazel and heads to a long, floral curtain hanging from the ceiling. Once she steps behind, the biddies start their clucking again.

"Babs," Edith whispers, her mind as aflutter as a ticker tape parade.

"What?" Barbara snaps, examining her reflection in a compact and finding it wanting.

"You don't s'pose she's the wife of that photographer from *Life* magazine Clarissa told you about, do ya?"

Barbara snaps her compact shut. Their eyes meet significantly.

~ ~ ~ ~ ~

An hour later, Barbara and Edith hover as Hazel combs Grace's hair into a shiny bouffant. Barbara leans in confidentially, meeting Grace's eyes in the mirror. "You've simply *got* to join the Disciples of Christ congregation and meet Reverend Steve."

"We just love Reverend Steve," sighs Edith. "He's got a

scandalous cleft chin, just like one of them men on the cover of a *Harlequin Romance* novel. Not that I read those things, I just see 'em in the checkout line at the grocers!"

"You are Protestant, aren't you, Grace? Can I call you Grace?" Barbara asks.

"Of course," Grace replies. "And we do adhere to Protestant scripture, mostly. I look forward to joining the church so we can become part of your wonderful community. My daughter, Maggie, had her first day at WaKeeney High yesterday."

"So *that's* your daughter!" exclaims Barbara.

"Well, I'll be hog-tied to a hitching post. I had no idea!" brays Edith.

Suddenly, the bell on Hazel's door tinkles alarmingly. In lurches Edith's husband, Len McCoy, wearing grimy coveralls and mud-caked boots, and clearly in a race to beat his wife in heft.

"Len McCoy, don't you know to leave those gull-derned boots outside? You're bringin' all the filth in here!" Edith scolds.

Len has years of practice at paying his wife no mind. His eyes fix on Hazel as he pulls off his cap. "Miss Atkins, I think I got that fence stabilized." He shifts on his feet. "You wanna come and have a looksee?"

"Oh, I'm sure it's fine, Mr. McCoy," Hazel says evenly.

Watching Len's eyes lingering on Hazel's form, Edith looks like she ate a raw lemon. "She doesn't have to check your work every step of the way, Len," she barks.

Len manages to pull his eyes toward his wife. "I just like to make sure my customers are satisfied, dear."

"Well, I guess she oughta be satisfied since you've been

workin' on her fence for damn-near six whole days when Jerry Unger's been needin' you for his barn loft all this time!" Edith cries.

Hazel looks up from Grace's hair, glancing from Len to Edith. "Then I don't want to hold him up," she assures. Wiping her hands on her apron, Hazel heads toward her tiny office. "Let me just get your money, Mr. McCoy."

Len's eyes follow Hazel out of the room. Truly, I've seen dogs with more dignity.

Barbara leans over to Grace, whispering just loud enough for Edith's ears, "You best be sure to keep your husband clear of Hazel. She's practically thirty and still not married! Pretty much every farmhand in WaKeeney acts like a rooster around her, 'cept my Henry, thank the stars."

"She needs to find herself a man to marry or get the hell out of Dodge," Edith grouses.

Grace smooths her skirt. "Sounds scandalous," she breathes, refusing to meet her own bootlicking eye in the mirror.

~ ~ ~ ~ ~

That night, standing in her pristine canary yellow kitchen, wearing a day dress too fancy for any family supper, Grace appraises her pot roast uncertainly.

Arranged amidst a crowd of plump peas on Grandma Ann's Wedgewood platter, the pot roast steams pleasantly, but Grace can't be sure it isn't dry.

Her husband, Gerald, is picky about his meat. If it's too rare, he feeds it to their springer spaniel, Max. Too dry and he throws it in the trash bin without a word.

Grace was extra careful this time. Checking the meat every fifteen minutes, probing the flesh to make sure it maintained the right shade of pink. A knight going into battle could not have prepared himself better.

Grace pats her newly coiffed hair. Thank goodness that's above reproach. Gerald likes to tell her, "The Greeks got it right. They believed that Beauty is a virtue as important as any other, including Piety, Humility and Kindness."

Gerald's never begrudged the dollars it takes to make Grace look perfect. (She often forgets they're *her* dollars, but Gerald never does.)

Grace carefully adds baby new potatoes to the pot roast arrangement, as well as fresh sprigs of rosemary cut from her recently-planted garden. Then she picks up the platter and bears it into the dining room like a military standard.

Gerald sits at the head of the table — bespectacled, silver-haired, and upright as a two-by-four. Maggie and her younger siblings, ten-year-old twins Emmet and Tallulah — currently in a violent thumb war — are already seated when Grace sets her platter before Gerald.

"Not pot roast again!" Emmet groans. "It tastes like tires!"

Gerald's jaw tightens. "You will not be rude to your mother, son," he warns.

Tallulah can't help but pile on. "Yeah, don't be rude, Emmett!"

Emmett leans his face over Tallulah's table setting, dangling a string of spit over her empty plate.

"Stop it, Emmett! That's disgusting!" Tallulah shrieks. "Mom, I need a new plate!"

Gerald's eyes go cold. "That's enough!" he growls in a voice that brooks no argument. "The two of you will eat like civilized human beings or go straight to bed on hungry stomachs."

The room falls silent. Emmett sneaks a look at Maggie. She winks at her brother as he slurps the spit back into his mouth.

Grace slides invisibly into a chair at the far end of her exquisitely set table. "I stopped by the local beauty salon today," she offers, with a hopeful smile. "I met a friendly woman named Barbara Dell who says her daughter Clarissa is in Maggie's chemistry class."

"Is that right?" Gerald mutters, delicately slicing the pot roast as Grace stiffens, awaiting his verdict on the meat.

"Yes! And this Clarissa is apparently quite popular," Grace continues, "She can help Maggie meet new friends, Barbara said. Really nice girls."

Maggie rolls her eyes. "I've already met some of those 'nice' girls, Mom, and they'll kill you with kindness."

"That's wonderful," Grace responds, choosing to ignore Maggie's true meaning. But Gerald eagle-eyes his daughter.

"It wouldn't hurt you to meet nice friends, Maggie. Good girls. Make the best of the situation." He stabs a thin slice of meat, putting it on his plate. "God knows, we're all trying to make the best of it here!"

A heavy silence descends. It could drag Grace six feet under, if she let it. Her heart breaks over the tension between Gerald and Maggie, especially when she remembers how warm and loving their relationship used to be.

Maggie loved her daddy so much as a small child that Grace was even jealous. Maggie always wanted "Daddy" to feed her, "Daddy" to rock her to sleep, "Daddy" to pick her up out of her crib.

It got so bad, Grace begged to have another child —

despite Gerald's insistence the world was already overpopulated — just so she could have one of her own. Then she got more than she bargained for with twins. Now Grace would give anything to make things between Gerald and Maggie the way they used to be.

Maggie looks cautiously at her parents, careful where to step. "I just hope the local girls will like me."

"*I* like you," Tallulah pipes up.

"I like you too, Lula-bee," Maggie smiles.

Gerald clears his throat, softening. "Let's put a lid on it and pray so we can enjoy your mother's delicious meal before it goes cold."

He reaches out and the Richmonds join hands, lower their heads and close their eyes. "Dear Heavenly Father …" Gerald begins.

As he drones on, Maggie's eyes open. She looks from one family member to the next as if she's watching from a train pulling from the station.

With each passing year, Maggie feels like she's picking up speed, moving away and away and away from them. She wonders how long it will be before her family's entirely out of view.

When Gerald's prayer ends, he takes a bite of the pot roast. Without a word, he spits it into his napkin and drops it on the floor for the dog.

~ ~ ~ ~ ~

It's ten o'clock on a Wednesday night. Francie and Hank Deerborne sit in their parlor. Francie pretends to watch television, but her eyes keep shifting to Hank, whose nose is buried in the *Hays Daily Chronicle*.

Francie's sour ruminations rattle around in her head and

my ears like a Tilt-a-Whirl at a carnival.

As far as she's concerned her life's as boring as mud. And when Francie's bored, she drinks. Well, Francie drinks even when she's not bored. But bored-drunk makes her meaner.

Using her index finger, Francie stirs the ice in her tumbler of Jim Beam. She tosses the rest of the whiskey back, her third of the evening.

The fact that Hank doesn't even look up makes her eye the liquor cabinet with a defiant thirst.

You'd never know Hank Deerborne was once a dreamy quarterback at Trego County High. That's when sixteen-year-old Francie lost her virginity to him in his mama's upstairs sewing room, while Hank's family had Sunday barbecue in the kitchen below.

Just her luck, Francie was pregnant before her feet hit the floor. But she didn't mind, because Hank was her gridiron superstar, with a promising career ahead of him.

After the shotgun wedding, she bragged to anyone who'd listen about all the bright-light cities she'd live in. Chicago. New York. Hell, anywhere that put miles of blacktop between her and this blink-and-you-miss-it outpost.

She even talked about the fortune she'd spend on furs and T-birds as her brawny husband threw rockets into the end zone.

And, oh! The "highfalutin'" people she'd entertain in her chic home! The vacations she'd take in ritzy places like London, Paris and the Italian Riviera — places she'd seen in the *Vogue* magazines she flipped through in the grocery line.

But the fancy talk stopped when disaster struck.

Hank tore a tendon in his calf and, just like that, he was off the football field and back on the family farm, driving a combine.

A seed of hate wedged itself inside Francie's heart then and grew as quick and ornery as crabgrass. Three months later came Iris. Their one and only daughter.

I remember that time, seeing Francie with tiny Iris. The way she'd nervously clutch that newborn as if someone handed her a can of gasoline and a lit match.

One month in, Francie left Iris in a bassinet and a note for Hank on the kitchen table. Seems a bible salesman by the name of Rusty Allred rang the doorbell earlier that day, his lanky frame leaning up against a porch pillar as if he owned the damn place.

Despite his cheap suit, scuffed two-tone oxfords and wolf's grin, that Rusty was a real looker. Within the hour, Francie had lit out of town in the passenger seat of Rusty's sputtering '58 Edsel.

Two days later there was a knock at my door. Ned answered. It was Hank and squalling Iris. I can still see Hank in the doorway — a child himself at just eighteen — his eyes full of fear and guilt.

Ned had been Hank's Lutheran Boy's advisor and had heard the full measure of Hank's sorrow for having "relations" with Francie before entering the sanctity of marriage.

Ned assured Hank there is no Hell, despite what the Protestants might think, but it was clear the young man had found Hell anyway. He begged us to take the baby. She needed a mother, he said, and his own mama was gone long ago with The Cancer.

Little Jeff was in one arm when I reached out for Iris with the other. I couldn't say no to Hank's desperation, becoming so well acquainted with it myself.

From that moment, both babies were together always. They slept face to face in one crib, breathing each other's soft breath. When one cried, the other would reach out in comfort.

For a time my Voices quieted, smothered by the hard, true love I had for those two babies.

Exactly one year to the day that Iris came into our home, there was another knock on my door. This time Francie Deerborne stood on my stoop. She had a split lip, fingerprint bruises on her upper arms and a faint purple-yellow bloomer hemming in her right eye.

Word around town said Rusty Allred was a bigamist with five wives in as many states. Moreover, he had a penchant for blackout drinking, so he never remembered laying hands on his women.

Evidently, though, he hadn't beaten the shrew out of Francie. Her eyes were cold as flint when she demanded her baby. *Her* baby!

Before I could even gather Iris's belongings, Francie snatched the child, howling, from my arms, turned on her heel and marched away. It was the last time I held that little girl.

For a while, Francie played penitent mother and model wife. We'd see her around town, pushing a carriage, linking arms with Hank, issuing the usual pleasantries.

But it wasn't long before we'd spot Francie driving off, slipping into bars. Wearing her skirts shorter, her sweaters tight, her face harder. And we wouldn't see Hank or Iris at all.

Francie's lot in life eventually turned her lemon-bitter. She accepted she'd never leave WaKeeney but took whatever pleasure she could out of tormenting the ones she held to account. And her husband was culprit Number One.

At the moment, Hank risks a furtive glance at his wife. Normally he'd be in bed by seven, given he's up at the cockcrow. But Hank doesn't like leaving Francie alone to drink.

It's not true, you know. Hank's not the failure Francie thinks he is. His deft way with cattle and crops has modestly supported the family through thick and thin. But around Francie, Hank folds up like a newborn calf.

Most of us think he should never have taken her back, not after she played him for a fool before the whole town. But I guess Hank's never understood that a wild woman isn't like a wild horse. There's no breaking this one.

Francie flicks a bleary gaze to *Playhouse 90* blaring from the Philco. Some World War II movie Hank put on. Cows and war being the stuff that lights that "dunderhead" up.

Easy-on-the-eyes James Mason plays a German spy trying to turn the tide of the war toward Hitler. Francie looks from Mason's firm, clean-shaven jaw to Hank's two-day stubble.

"I bet James Mason steers clear of steer," Francie slurs, chuckling at her own pun.

Hank sinks in his armchair and turns another page.

"Hey, you!" Francie says, "I'm talkin' to you!" She throws an ice cube at Hank, just missing his head.

His jaw tightens. "Leave it be, Francie," Hank warns.

"Leave it be, Francie," she mimics. Then tosses another ice cube. This one hits Hank's newspaper. Sighing, he shakes the paper out and tries to finish the one sentence he's already read ten times.

Seeing she's not getting a reaction, Francie loses interest. Bored, boring, boring-est. With a grunt she lurches onto her feet and zigzags for the booze cabinet. As she reaches inside for a bottle, Hank's paper goes down.

"That's enough for you," he says.

"It might be enough for you, but it sure as Shinola ain't enough for me."

Hank's had it. He shoots to his feet and goes for Francie, wrenching the bottle from her grip. "Goddammit, I told you, that's enough!"

Cool as you please, Francie just reaches for another bottle. Hank grabs her wrist.

"Don't you touch me!" Francie shouts. "Don't you ever touch me with those dirty manure hands! You think you own me? You don't own me. I could leave anytime. Any damn time I wanted!"

Hank's all adrenaline now. He starts jerking liquor bottles out of the cabinet.

"What're you doin'?" Francie sobers quick. Clearly the game's gone all wrong.

Hank marches for the kitchen sink with his capture.

"What the hell're you doin', Hank Deerborne? Don't you dare! Don't you dare pour my liquor out!"

Francie flies into the kitchen after him, hollering to beat the band.

~ ~ ~ ~ ~

The shouting reaches Iris upstairs in her bedroom. She squeezes her eyes shut tight. Presses her hands firmly over her ears, trying to block out the cursing and breaking glass.

After all these years, Iris would like to know why her parents' fights still make her breath come shallow, her Terrible Shame threaten?

Another bottle shatters. Francie's shrieks of rage boil up

through the floorboards.

Iris can't stand it another second. She throws off the covers and rolls out of bed, then slips on her glasses, jerks on a pair of work boots and makes for the window.

Quietly, Iris slides the window sash up and climbs out. As she has done over an ocean of years, Iris expertly crosses the roof below her bedroom window, grabs a branch of her trusty maple ash and shimmies down to her escape.

Once Iris's feet hit the ground, she picks up the hem of her nightgown and runs pell-mell through the nighttime fields.

~ ~ ~ ~ ~

As true as true can be, Sumner Pond waits patiently for Iris. A full harvest moon shines down on her velvety waters, lighting them up like a magical page from Iris's favorite book, *The Secret Garden*.

She feels Sumner Pond changes her the way *The Secret Garden* changed the lonely orphan, Mary Lennox, into someone beloved.

I wonder if Iris senses my ghostly presence in the place my soul lingers most dense. Does she know, this time, I won't let her go until she's safe?

Tonight, Iris crashes through the trees, hardly noticing the tiny cuts from branches and brambles on her face. Breathing raggedly, she charges into the water as if flames were chasing her.

The warm spring soaks Iris's nightgown. She welcomes its embrace and lets her head go under. Silence. Nothingness. Peace.

When Iris emerges she rolls onto her back to float. Slowly, slowly, her breathing calms. Her blood cools. Her thoughts quiet. On land, water is the enemy. But here, at Sumner Pond, it's a cocoon. Making her weightless, free. That is, until a bomb drops.

KARRASSSHHHHH!

A mighty splash shocks Iris's eyes open. She flounders to her feet, back-pedaling toward shore. Someone or some*thing* has just jumped into the pond with her!

Iris prays it isn't anything that bites. Her daddy had mentioned a band of coyotes wilding across the land. They slaughtered Len McCoy's sheep, Coretta Bayleaf's chickens and Mrs. Stradall's Jack Russell Terrier, Fred.

But no. The next sound is a very human, "WhoooOOOOP!"

Iris squints in the dark. "Who is it? Who's there?" she shouts, her voice quaking with indignation.

"It's Maggie!"

"Who?"

The interloper dog-paddles closer so Iris can see her. "Maggie Richmond."

"How … why … what're you doing here?!"

"Swimming," Maggie replies, as if stating the obvious.

"This is a private place!" Iris hisses, still stunned by this turn of events.

"I didn't know a pond could be private," Maggie says, adding a cool edge to her voice. "And if it's so private, what're you doing here?"

Iris is momentarily speechless.

"If it's so private," Maggie repeats, "how come you're here?"

"'Cuz it's my place," Iris replies, mulish.

"Do you own it?"

"Well, no."

"Then how's it yours?"

"It just is."

"Mind if I use it for a while?"

Arms folded, chin jutting, Iris clearly minds. She opens her mouth to say so when she notices something outrageous. "You're naked!" Iris hisses. "You shouldn't be naked! What if someone sees you?"

Maggie snorts. "I thought you said this place was private? Besides you, who's gonna see me?"

Iris doesn't have a good answer for that, but Maggie's presence infuriates her more and more with each passing second. How dare the new girl swim in her pond, and naked to boot? That's when Iris gets an idea, a new card to play. "You better be careful," she warns.

"Why?" Maggie asks, a thread of worry climbing her spine.

Iris points down at the water, almost casually. "There's a dead body in here."

Well played, Iris, I think. *Well played.*

"Whose body?" Maggie asks with a shudder that gives Iris a great deal of satisfaction.

"Charlotte Owings."

Maggie edges toward the shore, not too slowly. "What happened? Did she drown?"

Iris nods. "She did it on purpose ... suicide. Walked right in 'till the water covered her head and never came out again. They haven't found the body 'cuz there's underwater caves and aquifers down there. It's probably stuck in one of 'em.

61

Anyway, that's why no one comes here."

Now, if I were the oral historian of my own demise, I'd make it a bit more poetic:

> *"Charlotte Owings — a highly-educated, brilliant but tortured woman — sunk herself, as Virginia Woolf did in the River Ouse, with heavy rocks sewed into the lining of her sturdiest woolen coat. Those same rocks now press what's left of her body and restless soul into the silty, mysterious, alchemistic bottom of Summer Pond."*

That just sits better with me.

"Why'd she kill herself?" Maggie asks.

Iris starts to open her mouth, but no answer comes. Instead, her eyes cloud with the memory of the last time she saw me alive.

It was blazing hot that June of '51. I stood outside the doors of The Bethel Street Lutheran Church in my buttoned-up, stone-lined coat, pining to sneak inside and steal one last look at my boy, Jeff. Even if it was just the back of his head. Those wayward cowlicks I loved so well.

But my feet would not move. Sweat poured down my face. My heart was heavy with the certainty my son would be better off without me. It's clear to me now that the mother of a small boy shouldn't do herself in. But nothing was clear to me then.

Some days were black and soundless, like the inside of a filled-to-the-brim grain silo. Other days the Voices made me feel like I was going to explode from the inside out.

During these times — well, three of them exactly — I drove down to Hays, the nearest big city, and found myself a traveling-gentleman type a married woman should avoid.

Ned knew. He was a soft-hearted man who forgave me,

each time, because he sensed something inside of me was sick. It was my broken brain, not my heart, that separated me from my husband. From everything. Including my son.

Just as I turned to flee the church where my family sat inside, the doors burst open and seven-year-old Iris stumbled out. Her face was a twist of mortification, the front of her dress drenched from waist to hem — the first time her Terrible Shame struck.

We were brought up short by each other. She three steps above. Me three steps below.

Our eyes collided for the first time since Francie wrenched her from my arms. I had never sought her out, never looked for her in a crowd of children. I could not bear the soul-crushing loss of her.

There in the wavery high-noon heat, outside the church, I was struck by the notion we each had a solar system in our heads, with a million tiny interconnections, orbits and constellations spinning beyond our control. Clashing, colliding, vacuum-sucked into unknowable black holes.

But when our eyes locked, so did our orbits. Our separate solar systems ground to a halt, suspended for that moment in eternity.

Iris was no longer the child ripped from my side. I was no longer the crazy lady she didn't remember as her first nurturer. We recognized ourselves in each other. Fear knowing fear. Pain knowing pain.

Then Iris broke away, no longer able to look into the soul of a woman flattened by the truck of her sadness. And I went to the pond.

"Why'd Charlotte Owings kill herself?" Maggie prods again, floating in the water next to Iris under the man-in-the-moon.

Iris leans back, letting her hair drift.

"At first, I thought it was 'cuz people said mean things about her," she replies softly. "'Cuz she did things married women weren't s'posed to do. But now ... I think she just couldn't stop being sad."

The girls fall quiet, sinking deeper into the water as the night air turns chilly.

"Maybe I should kill myself then," Maggie says abruptly. "Lie down on the bottom of the pond with Charlotte Owings."

Iris turns on Maggie. "That's not funny! She was really sad, not like you!"

"What do you know about me?" Even in the dark, Maggie's face has gone angry-red.

Iris clamps her mouth shut. First this strange, stunning girl everyone wants in their crowd crashes into Iris's life at a humiliating moment and now this? The one place in the world Iris feels she can be herself and she's trespassing here too?!

Suddenly, Maggie shrieks like the Banshee of Ballyliffin.

"What is it?" Iris gasps, backing away.

"Someone's got my foot!" Maggie yells, thrashing about.

"They do not!"

Maggie flails violently. "It's Charlotte Owings! She's got me! She's got me by the foot! Oh, my God! Oh, my ..!"

Maggie's head disappears under water.

"Maggie?" Iris fights for calm in the silence. The water stills where Maggie submerged. Nothing moves. "Maggie?" Iris whispers, "quit fooling around!"

The flat, black water won't answer.

"Maggie?" Iris pleads. Terrified, she backs toward shore, inch by inch, when, abruptly, she's pulled under too with a shriek.

Silence. Faint ripples and tiny air bubbles pop, pop, pop on the indifferent surface of the water.

Suddenly, Iris spouts out of the water, screaming until something jerks her under again. Seconds go by, then, all at once, both girls surface, sputtering and spitting. Iris flails at Maggie, shrieking, "Help! Help!"

Maggie can take no more. She roars with laughter.

In a split second, Iris shifts from realization to relief to fuming rage. "That's not funny!" she shouts.

"You didn't see your face. It was hilarious!"

Iris turns on Maggie, spitting words. "You're no better than the rest of 'em, lookin' to feel big by steppin' on somebody else!"

She makes for shore as fast as she can until her soaked nightgown tangles around her ankles making her stumble. Another humiliation.

Maggie cries out. "Wait! Don't go! This is your place."

"You ruined it!"

"Please," Maggie begs. "Please, don't go!"

The urgency in Maggie's voice stops Iris. She turns back. Maggie's luminous features are rent with astonishing loneliness.

"Please, don't go," Maggie whispers. "We could share it."

It occurs to Iris that maybe beautiful people can be broken too.

~ ~ ~ ~ ~

"And then they wanted me to be a fashion model ..."

Maggie is mid-tale as both girls sit drip-drying on the shore.

To Iris's evident relief, Maggie wears the nightgown she laid out before her skinny-dip.

"But my daddy didn't want me to be a model in case I'd get conceited," Maggie continues, hugging her shins. "'Cuz he works with those famous actresses all the time and sees how conceited they get. But I did take a few modeling classes. You wanna learn how to sell lips?"

Iris considers Maggie, confused. "Sell ... lips?"

"Yeah. See, let's say you're a model for lipstick? You gotta know how to sell lips. Here. Watch me."

Maggie pooches out her lips as if she was trying to whistle. Or upchuck.

"Do you feel okay?" Iris asks.

"I'm selling lips!" Maggie demonstrates again, "Now you try it."

Iris stares at Maggie like she's trying to figure an equation. "You're a liar," she blurts before her brain can filter her mouth.

Maggie goes still. "What?"

"Nothin'. Never mind."

"What'd you say?" Maggie insists.

"I'm ... it's just ... I'm sorry. It's just I noticed ... you lie. You did it in chemistry the other morning. Your daddy doesn't work for *Life* magazine."

Maggie huffs. "'Course, he does!"

"And you didn't take model classes neither."

"I did too! What do you know?" Maggie glares at the trees.

Iris is careful. "Nothin'. I could just tell, that's all. I didn't mean anythin' by it. Maybe you just ..." she shrugs, "... want people to like you?"

Maggie turns on Iris, stung. "Why do you think that? 'Cuz that's what you want? 'Cuz you wish they'd like you?" Maggie's voice is rising.

"I ... I don't wish they'd like me," Iris sputters. "I just wish they'd leave me alone."

Maggie jumps to her feet, furious.

"You don't know me! You don't know anything about me, 'cept for one thing. You're right. I *am* a liar. I lied about wantin' to share this pond with you. You can have it!"

Then Maggie's gone like a flash through the trees leaving Iris to wonder how it is that each time she encounters the new girl, she's left speechless.

~ ~ ~ ~ ~

Shivering in her wet hair, Maggie sneaks across her yard to the front porch, hoping Grace, who oft-times can't sleep, didn't come downstairs and lock the front door.

Maggie's thoughts stop cold when a shadow unfolds from the porch swing.

It's Gerald. Fully dressed, her father steps deliberately into her path, a leather belt hanging loose in his grip. "I looked all over town for you the last two hours," he says.

Maggie shrinks. "Sorry, Daddy."

"Who were you with?" Gerald asks coolly.

Maggie takes two steps back. "No one."

A light comes on downstairs. The front door edges open. "Maggie?" Grace's head appears. "Maggie? Is that you, sweetie?"

Maggie wonders why her mother looks so well-groomed at two in the morning. Hair in perfect pin curls. Lace night gown and floral robe pristine.

"Get back inside, Grace," Gerald orders.

"Honey, it's late," Grace murmurs, "Wouldn't it be best if we all came in?"

"Grace!" Gerald barks.

She whispers to Maggie, "You had us so worried … so, so worried."

A moment of stillness descends upon Grace. A hint of something hard lodges in her belly as she looks at her husband.

"Grace," Gerald says once more. Quiet as death.

The hardness seeps out of Grace, replaced with resignation. She pulls her head back into the house, softly closing the door behind her.

Gerald turns to Maggie. "I'm going to ask you one more time, who were you with?"

Maggie lifts her chin and stares Gerald down. "I went swimming. Alone."

Before her mouth can close, Gerald strikes.

Crack! Crack! Crack! The belt whips across Maggie's chest, her shoulder, the side of her head. Welts sprout like flung paint.

It's over in seconds. Then the pain comes on hard, a million wasp stings where Gerald lashed her. Fists clenched, Maggie bites back sobs. She refuses to let her father see her cry.

Gerald breathes hard. His voice shakes when he says, "I left my job for you. Moved the entire family for you. Tallulah looks up to you. She wants to *be* like you!"

"You already told me that," Maggie's gone dead calm. Gerald's done his worst. She's moved past him. He can't hurt her now.

"We won't do it again," Gerald threatens. "Next time, we'll go without you. We'll leave you behind."

"I said … it won't happen again."

His rage spent, Gerald steps aside. "Get inside and dry yourself off."

Maggie straightens her spine and walks past her father like a gladiator leaving the ring.

When his daughter is gone, Gerald sags against the porch pillar. He takes several unsteady breaths, then refastens his belt and follows Maggie inside.

Chapter Four

Iris trudges along Old Junction Road like a prisoner-of-war in the Bataan Death March, accursed by the infernal Indian Summer heat.

At the wheel of her Packard, Maggie Richmond follows. The stomp of Iris's feet syncopates with the hum of the engine.

The two girls maintain this creeping pas de deux for nigh on a mile, Iris refusing to slow or look back and Maggie refusing to look away.

Without warning, Iris halts like a mule in its furrow. Maggie leans on the brakes, letting the car idle.

Iris turns and stares at Maggie through the windshield. A decision is made. Iris marches to the Packard, opens the passenger door and climbs in, slamming the door shut.

The two girls, taut as catgut strings, sit in silence. Maggie slides her foot onto the gas pedal and eases her car down the road, worried that if she makes just one false move, Iris will edge her door open and roll out of the moving car.

For her part, Iris sneaks a look at Maggie. She notices a dark bruise empurpling Maggie's right temple.

"What's that?" she asks.

Maggie drives. After a moment, Maggie asks Iris, "How come they call you Stinky Drawers?"

Iris stares straight ahead at the never-changing road. A stalemate.

~ ~ ~ ~ ~

Clarissa Dell and Rhonda Robertson perch like high-strung Persians in a strategic location in the senior's student

70

parking lot, where all the Big Men On Campus park.

It's the absolute, most advantageous spot to be seen by them. Prom is on the horizon and the Songbirds will be strung up over the fires of Hades before they go with someone from the marching band!

Hearing a motor thrum, Clarissa looks up from her compact, readying herself for a possible drive-by swain. But no. Instead, an ignominious vision assaults her sense of well-being.

"Sweet Mother of God, *what* does she think she's doin'?" Clarissa exclaims.

"Who? What? *Where?*" Rhonda rubbernecks.

"Rhonda, open your eyes! Maggie Richmond's parking in the boy's section, of all things, and ..." she squints at the car. "No, no, please let my eyes be deceivin' me!"

"What is it?" Rhonda presses.

"Can't you see who's riding with her?"

Rhonda gathers all her faculties of discernment to identify Maggie's co-pilot. Then, as if it's of no account, "Iris Deerborne's in her car."

"Exactly!" Clarissa glares at Rhonda's halfwit face. "Don't you get it?"

"Get what?"

Not for the first time, Clarissa wonders why in tarnation she's friends with such a blundering moron.

"Rhonda, Maggie is, right before our very eyes, committing social suicide. She might be from the city, but that girl needs schoolin'!"

Clarissa grabs Rhonda by the arm and pulls her away. "We gotta rally the troops!"

~ ~ ~ ~ ~

Maggie studies her reflection in the girls' locker room mirror. It's not her usual self she sees fidgeting in a too-short tartan skirt and Little Bo Peep white blouse — the official Songbird uniform.

Maggie yanks the skirt down to cover more of her long legs, while the rest of the Songbirds change from their civvies into their uniforms.

She watches thoughtfully as the other girls adjust garters and petticoats, apply make-up, and shellac bouffant hair-dos with Aqua Net.

There's some perplexity in her face, as if Maggie's trying to measure the enormous distance between her battered self and these "normal" girls. To her they don't seem to have a care in the world.

Of course, I could tell her a thing or two about these "normal" girls.

For instance, Betty Drury makes herself vomit up dinner every night in the guest powder room. Her mom, Lidia, has entered Betty in beauty pageants since she could walk. After all the painting, prodding and preening, purging food from her body is the only thing that makes Betty feel like she's got a say in her own life.

Then there's Sally Jenkins, who's is in love with Mr. Ben Whitman. Sally babysits his and Mrs. Whitman's children every Saturday night at fifteen cents an hour.

Last Saturday, when Mr. Whitman was driving Sally home, he pulled over to the side of the road and kissed her. In the very moment her heart soared, Mr. Whitman said it was a mistake and could never happen again. But Sally got the feeling it might.

And, as it turns out, Shayla Lyons, who'd put on a substantial amount of weight last summer, wasn't on a special internship in the nation's capital, Washington D.C. In reality, she left a seven-pound, five-ounce bundle of joy with a barren couple there.

Shayla thinks about that little swaddled package most every single day.

Maybe if Maggie knew these secrets, she wouldn't feel so alone in a crowded room.

Clarissa and Rhonda finish donning their close-fitting Songbird uniforms as their chatty, plump friend, Hattie McCoy, adjusts her substantial cleavage in a double F-cup Maidenform brassiere.

"Now Maggie," Hattie says, "don't be worried if you can't do the splits in tryouts. Mrs. Hibbard won't count that against you, so long as you've got flexibility in *other* areas. There's flexibility besides the splits."

"And you oughta know, Hattie," Clarissa teases.

Hattie whirls on her. "You don't have to be such a bitch, Clarissa!"

Yep, that's Edith's daughter: a McCoy who says what she means and means what she says.

Rhonda sits down next to Maggie and takes her hand. "And you absolutely *must* go to the School Spirit After-Game dance tomorrow night!"

"It's a good time to nail down a prom date," Clarissa chimes in. "It'll be here before we know it! And if you don't have a date to prom, you may as well wear a sign on your back that says 'Leper' on it."

Maggie tries for an expression of interest. "When does this event of great import take place?" she asks.

Clarissa doesn't like the tone of Maggie's voice. "Margot Richmond, I suggest you take the prom seriously. It's in just five short weeks! The first of November!"

"And let me tell you," Hattie warns, as she attempts buttoning her ever-tighter Songbird skirt, "The pickin's is gettin' miiiiiighty slim. Todd Ingram and Jerry Watson are already off the market! There's an air of hysteria building."

Clarissa sniffs. "Well, I'm not worried about myself. I've already turned Ernie Gomez down," she says. "He's half-beaner and in the Glee Club, for Godsakes. I mean, what was he thinking, asking me?"

Clarissa turns to Maggie, "But this is a crucial time for you. You can't afford to be lazy. We Songbirds always say, 'You gotta be great to get a fun date!'"

"I came up with that motto," Rhonda tells Maggie.

"You did not, Rhonda, as I can prove to you by the date I wrote it in my *Girl's Best Friend* diary," Hattie insists.

"The point is," Clarissa interrupts, warming to her cause, "You could get left home."

Clarissa sits down on the opposite side of Maggie, bookending her with Rhonda, and takes her other hand. "There's something we have to tell you."

Hattie draws close as the three girls form a ring around their recruit.

"We understand you're new and all ..." Clarissa grants.

"And there's no way you could know ..." Rhonda continues.

"But here's the thing. And I need you to listen closely," Clarissa intones. "It is essential — absolutely *essential* — that you stay away from Iris Deerborne."

"She's an Untouchable," Hattie whispers.

"An … Untouchable?" Maggie's brow furrows.

"Like in India," Rhonda explains. "We learned about it sophomore year in our Ancient Civilizations class? They're the lowest caste and bathe in their own body waste."

"Could you please not say that when I need to eat my late afternoon snack?" complains Hattie, who's already unwrapping a pink-frosted cruller from Finch's Bakery.

"I'm sure you'll still be able to choke it down," snipes Clarissa.

"I'll have you know I've lost five pounds this month!" Hattie cries.

"And you'll have them back on by Tuesday." Clarissa's voice rises to schoolmarm level. "Songbirds need to set an example, Hattie. We must have a little self-control!"

"We can't all be perfect like you!" Hattie huffs. She grabs her pom-poms and her donut then flounces out of the building.

Clarissa turns back to Maggie, the project at hand.

"You should know, bein' seen with Iris will be the death of your reputation in WaKeeney, and we'd hate for that to happen to a girl of your caliber."

"I see." Maggie sits poker-faced, her near-black eyes impossible to read. So why is it Clarissa's pretty sure Maggie's about to slap her?

Instead, the new girl smiles like spring-time sun coming out from behind winter clouds.

"Thanks for the warning, girls," Maggie declares. Then she gamely leaps to her feet and takes a cheerleader stance, pom-poms on hips.

Executing an array of impressive arm movements and acrobatic jumps WaKeeney's cheer coach has yet to discover,

Maggie shouts, "Ready, okay! Cheer for the Panthers! Cheer for the win! C'mon crowd yell, Go Fight Win!"

"How's that?" she asks the girls.

Clarissa snaps her jealous gaze away. "It needs work," she says dryly. "Let's go."

Rhonda turns to Maggie, "Do you think your dad'd photograph any of the games if you made squad?"

As the three girls file out of the locker room, they don't see Iris flattened against a nearby wall, the hot, shameful liquid rolling down her thighs.

~ ~ ~ ~ ~

The next afternoon, my son Jeff washes his hands at the water pump outside the Deerborne barn, done with his day's work.

He's at the farm both mornings and afternoons now. Arriving at the cock's crow, working two solid hours, then riding Ned's old beat-up Triumph Thunderbird motorbike to school.

Jeff doesn't have much use for school anymore. I was the one who read to him every night before lights-out and wrote stories for him about pirates and blaggards who'd sooner slit your throat than buckle their shoes.

Those stories came from the side of my brain that was full of fast, big, blooming, joyful thoughts — and education, too. After all, I'd gone four years to Hays State at a time most WaKeeney girls were busy filling their hope chests.

My stories made Jeff dream of college. He would've been the first man in our family to go. But my death, and later Ned's passing from a bad ticker, crushed that dream.

So Jeff's decided to become a farmer like Hank Deerborne. It's straightforward, uncomplicated work. For one thing, animals are more predictable than humans. They're not going to blindside you. If you treat them right, they'll return the favor.

Besides, the hard work helps Jeff set aside his grief. And Hank treats him like a son. It seems like Hank and I have come full circle. I took care of his baby long ago. Now, he's taking care of mine.

Just then, the kitchen screen door creaks open. Jeff looks up to see Francie leaning in the doorway, a hi-ball of scotch in one hand, her perennial cigarette in the other.

Jeff knows it's not just Iris who watches him.

It's true that town folks don't wag their tongues much about Francie and that bible salesman anymore. They immediately cut her more slack than me 'cuz Francie's meaner than a copperhead, and no one wanted to find themselves on the wrong end of those venomous fangs.

But Francie's wild past and still-good looks keep a lot of boys around here on their toes. There's plenty Jeff's age who think she's a "hot piece of tail," and speculate on all the ways Francie could teach them a thing or two about life.

Thank the Lord Jeff's not one of those boys. To him, she's just one more loose caboose who could send him through life sideways.

Cleaning up now, Jeff pretends he doesn't see Francie in her tight white blouse and snug navy-striped pedal pushers. Instead, he quickly straddles his motorbike and tries jump, jump, jumping it to life.

Francie ditches her drink on the porch railing and weaves her way through invisible obstacles to get to Jeff.

Sweat breaks out on Jeff's forehead when Francie touches the pillion seat just behind him. "This thing seats two!" she exclaims like she's discovered fire.

"Not easy," Jeff says, jumping on the starter pedal for all he's worth.

"I never said I was easy, young man," Francie teases.

"I didn't mean it like that," Jeff replies, coloring.

"I know what you meant." Francie's smile shifts to something predatory. "How 'bout you give me a ride anyways?"

"I gotta go, Mrs. Deerborne. My gran's expectin' me for dinner."

"Why don't you just take me for a quick spin to get the wind in my hair."

"Mr. Deerborne wouldn't like it."

That wipes the smile off Francie's face. "Oh, Hank. Hank's out in the back forty tonight with his cows. Moonin' on his cows." Francie's voice softens with promise. "Come on, honey, I'm payin' for the gas in this bike, I may as well get a ride on it."

Francie unsteadily throws a leg over the seat behind Jeff, pressing her chest against his back, wrapping her arms around his waist.

"Mrs. Deerborne, this is a bad idea." Jeff shrugs hard and jumps off the bike.

Francie grabs at his sleeve. "Oh no, you don't! You don't gotta go. Hey!"

In a split-second she's drunk-ugly. As she lurches off the seat, the bike topples to the ground at Jeff's feet. He backs up several paces, weighing the consequences of running for it.

Francie sees him slipping away. "You stop right there!

Come back and give me a ride!" she demands, moving up on Jeff.

"Mrs. Deerborne," Jeff says, hands out in front of him, trying to ward her off, "I think you'd feel better if you went inside."

"I don't wanna go inside. I wanna go for a ride!" Francie clutches at Jeff's shirt, presses herself against his young chest. "Just 'cuz your crazy mama killed herself don't mean you have to be scared of *every* woman you meet!" she cries.

I'm gratified when Jeff recoils from Francie like he's snake bit. Until he steps right smack into Iris, who's rounded the corner carrying a basket full of fresh eggs from the coop.

"Oh, no!" Jeff shouts as Iris flails backward, trying with all her might not to fall.

But Lady Luck's not on Iris's side today. Her feet go skyward, landing her hard on her backside. The egg basket catapults into the air, sending its oval torpedoes flying until they plummet back to earth like yolk-laden hail.

Splat! Splat! Splat! Splat! Each egg ruptures on top of Iris, leaving a puddled, oozing mess in her hair and lap. "I'm … I'm so sorry, Mama!" Iris cries, scrambling to scoop up the broken, slimy bits and pieces.

"Fat lot of good that'll do us when we wanna eat an omelet tomorrow," Francie complains.

Jeff kneels next to Iris. He's trying to help her clean up when their hands collide, making her drop more eggs from sheer nerves.

"Iris, you need to calm down, sweetheart. You get close to a good-lookin' boy and you just fall all to pieces." Francie gives Iris a sour grin.

Mortified, Iris drops one last egg.

"Just leave it, Iris!" Francie's dulcet tone drips with poison. "They're all ruined anyways. Let the dog get 'em. Now, go on inside before you make matters worse!"

Iris can't swallow the ragged sob that escapes her as she drops the basket and runs for the house. The back door slams shut behind her.

"That'll come out of your allowance!" Francie shouts after Iris.

Jeff's hands ball into fists. My boy wants to knock the words back down Mrs. Deerborne's throat, follow Iris into the house and tell her that woman isn't worth even one of her tears. But he's not quite the man for that. Not yet. He needs the job at the Deerbornes, so Jeff grabs his bike off the ground and climbs on.

Once he gets the engine started, though, he looks Francie dead in the eye. "Take the egg money out of my wages."

As Jeff roars off, Francie stares after him, a harsh, unfulfilled ache in her chest.

~ ~ ~ ~ ~

That night, Iris hunkers down with the bed covers pulled over her head. She rolls up into a tight ball, clutching a small transistor radio to her ear.

Skeeter Davis sings, "My Last Date With You":

"One hour and I'll be meeting you — I know you're gonna make me blue — My heart is trembling through and through — 'Cuz I know very well — I can tell — I can tell — This will be my last date with you."

Iris relaxes as she hears the lament in Skeeter's voice. It somehow eases her own pain.

For a moment, she closes her eyes and lets her legs stretch out, toes tickling under the covers.

As the last notes fade and Del Shannon starts singing "Runaway," Iris's bedroom crashes open. She doesn't have to look to know that Francie's silhouette sags in the door frame. Heart pounding, Iris snuffs the radio and hides it under her pillow like contraband.

Francie snaps on the bedroom light. She's blind drunk and clutching her handmade, calamitous prom dress. Francie thrusts the vulgarity at her daughter.

"Try this on, Iris. This is your Boy Catcher. You gotta know how to catch the boys. Come on, get up. Try on your Boy Catcher!"

Iris gathers the bedcovers under her chin, trying to find a soft exit from this new bout of madness. "Mama, I'm too tired. I was sleeping."

Francie's not having it. She grabs at Iris.

"Get up, get up, get up! Do you know how sick n' tired I am of people in this town lookin' down on you? I want more for you than that."

She pulls Iris upright. "When I was your age, I had to beat 'em off with a stick. I coulda got anybody. If I hadn't of got pregnant, who knows where I might be?!"

Iris hunches away from Francie, floundering for an escape.

"It's the middle of the night, Mama. You should go to bed."

"I could be livin' in the city now. A doctor's or lawyer's wife! Not stuck on some damn pig farm."

With that, Francie shoves the dress over Iris's head.

"You're not gonna miss your chance," she says, jerking the dress down over the nightgown. "No sir, not you, Iris!"

She spins her daughter around. Forces the zipper up in

back, then moves Iris in front of the mirror. Francie meets Iris's eyes with bleary pride. "There. Now, ain't that pretty?"

Iris looks at her bare feet. *Let me disappear. Let me disappear. Let me disappear.*

"What's the matter," Francie asks, for a moment perfectly sober. "Did you wet yourself?"

Iris looks up and sees the sharp blade of anticipation in Francie's eyes.

Suddenly the air in the room shifts. "Woman, get out of this room *right now* or so help me God, I'll tan your hide!"

Hank stands in the doorframe, clenched fists at his sides. He's never hit Francie. Not yet. But drunk as she is, Francie knows she's bumping up against his limit right now.

Francie lets Iris go. It takes a hot second for her to stop seeing double and get her bearings, but once she's got them, Francie defiantly crosses the room, squeezing past Hank, and disappears into the dark hallway without another word.

Hank turns worn-down eyes on his daughter, who's now a frightened heap on the bedclothes.

"I'm sorry, Bird," he says, softly. And for a second it seems like he's going to say something more … *do* something more. But the moment passes and Iris's daddy is gone with a muted click as the door closes behind him.

~ ~ ~ ~ ~

Iris runs.

She flies through broken wheat fields in the pink tulle abomination, stumbling on broken stalks, picking herself up again and running like the devil's at her heels.

Panting and sweating, Iris lurches through the ash trees into the clearing at Sumner Pond and falls to her knees. Sobs break through, raging and ragged. Rivers bursting dams.

She's spent and wrecked by the time Iris realizes she's not alone.

"Are you okay?"

Iris chokes and leaps up, dashing the tears from her face. A few yards away, Maggie Richmond gets to her feet.

"Don't come near me!" Iris shouts. "You don't wanna get near me!" She can't catch her breath, hyperventilating in huge, scary gasps.

Maggie, her face carefully neutral, inches closer, hands held out, as if she were approaching a frightened animal.

"I just wanna make sure you're okay," she says quietly. "Then I'll go."

"Get back!" Iris cries.

"It's okay."

"Get back!"

"It's okay."

"Please …" Iris collapses to the ground again. "I wet myself."

"What?"

Louder. "I wet myself."

"Oh."

Iris bows her head over her knees and lets the tears roll down her shins. Humiliating as it is, at least she can breathe again.

Maggie crouches near Iris, but not too close. Except for some fitful sobs from Iris, the two girls go quiet for a stretch, watching the glistening water eddy and drift.

Inside this solitude, Maggie makes a decision.

"My dad doesn't work for *Life* magazine," she admits.

"He works for *Agriculture Weekly*. He never took any pictures of Marilyn Monroe. He takes pictures of drainage pipes and cow piles."

Iris stares at Maggie, eyes big as platters.

"I never could've modeled neither. I'm too flat-chested," Maggie confesses. "And they never interviewed me for airline hostess. I couldn't be an airline hostess."

"Why not?" Iris breathes.

"I get airsick. Last time I was on an airplane, I puked my Ovaltine up in the aisle and the airline hostess made me clean it up myself. They're all first-class bitches."

Iris wipes her nose on her sleeve. "They call me Stinky Drawers 'cuz I wet myself when I'm nervous. Now you know why I'm an Untouchable. I heard them tell you … in the locker room."

Maggie's mortification outdoes Iris's. Her silence in the face of that cruelty makes her ashamed.

"Well, any name girls like Clarissa and Rhonda call you is a compliment," Maggie decrees. "You always gotta consider the source. Anything else I need to know?"

"Yes," Iris sobs. "I hate this stupid, *goddammed* dress!"

~ ~ ~ ~ ~

Francie's homespun atrocity floats on the shimmering surface of Sumner Pond like a ballooning pink fungus. The dress bobs briefly unmolested until, *kerplunk!* A heavy stone hits it dead center and it begins to sink.

On the shore, Maggie and Iris, now wearing just her nightgown, launch stone missiles at the dress. Maggie's second rock hits the bullseye, but Iris's rock goes wild.

"Whoa there, lefty," Maggie grins. "You gotta great arm, but the aim's a problem. Here's a technique for accuracy I learned from our greatest living southpaw, Bud Daley."

She picks up a rock and ratchets her arm back, young David aiming for Goliath.

"You point your free hand to where you want the rock to go, then fire it off with your throwing hand."

With her left index finger, Maggie points to the prom dress, then hurls the rock in her right hand with all her might. It strikes its target handily.

Iris gives it a go. Snatching up a rock, she points her right hand, drawing back her left, as Maggie does her best Russ Hodges' sportscasting play-by-play through her "hand" microphone.

"And Iris Deerborne takes the mound. This rookie's havin' one hell of-a season. Pitching six shutouts back to back. Here's the wind-up! And the release!"

Iris heaves her rock. *Splash!*

"It's a strikeout!" Maggie cheers as Iris's rock hits its target. "And the crowd goes wild!"

The girls dance, hoot and holler as Francie's hellish creation disappears into the drink with a final salute of pink lace fringe.

Iris watches gleefully, then feels something entirely unfamiliar. Triumph. A veritable parade of it, with trumpets, banners and hats thrown in the air.

When she glances at Maggie, though, all she can manage is a shy grin. "You sure do have a way with rocks."

~ ~ ~ ~ ~

As the clock chimes ten in the darkened homes of WaKeeney, Francie Deerborne furtively sips from a flask Hank doesn't know about near the jacaranda bush in the pitch-black of the back porch, her cigarette a nefarious pinpoint in the night.

One mile away, after the telephone hasn't rung once all night with a prom invite, Clarissa Dell devours two Hershey's chocolate bars from the stash her mama hides in the kitchen pantry.

In her bedroom two blocks over, Hattie McCoy attempts twenty sit-ups, but collapses exhausted and discouraged after just six.

She keeps her eyes averted from the *Seventeen* magazine on the floor, with its cover of slender girls in ski outfits.

Not for the first time, Hattie wishes she lived in the Rubens era, where rolls of flesh meant wealth and beauty.

On the north side of town, my Jeff sleeps in a twin bed across the hall from Ned's mom, Grandma Gini, whose chainsaw snores fail to wake him from a glorious dream.

He's racing a state-of-the-art Triumph Bonneville T120 at the Grand Prix. In the throng, his father and I cheer him on to a win. Sweet boy.

Two doors down, Grace Richmond lies in bed next to Gerald. He sleeps on his side. His back to her.

Grace has always loved the back of Gerald's neck. It's like the neck of a very young boy; soft, hairless, tender.

It takes all Grace's will not to reach out and touch it.

One field over, at Sumner Pond, two bodies float tranquilly side-by-side in the shallows.

Maggie has stripped nude, as is her wont, while Iris's white nightgown envelops her like bedsheets, the pond washing away her Terrible Shame.

"You don't have to talk to me at school," Iris says. "I'll understand."

Maggie's silent a moment. Her self-loathing grows with the length of that silence.

"It's 'cuz of my parents, the cheerleading and stuff. They need me to be ... *impressive.*'

"I understand."

"They hate me," Maggie murmurs.

"Who?"

"My parents."

Iris rolls to her feet, peering at Maggie to see if she's joking. But Maggie's somber face tells Iris she's not.

"Sometimes I wonder if they even see me."

"How could they not see you?" Iris responds. "You shine."

Maggie's throat goes tight. She turns her head from Iris's kind gaze.

"Let me pull you," Iris offers.

"Pull me?"

"Yeah. My daddy used to do this with me before the pond got haunted. It made me feel ... I don't know ... calmer somehow."

"Okay."

Iris stands as Maggie floats. She takes Maggie's right hand and gently pulls Maggie's body through the warm water.

Suddenly, a shooting star dances across the sky above them. Iris greets it as if it were an invited guest. She makes a wish out loud.

"If I had one wish, I'd wish to be like you, Maggie Richmond. Just for one day."

She continues drawing languid figure eights with Maggie's

body, her new friend's porcelain skin alight in the deep, dark black.

Chapter Five

I'm experiencing the great misfortune of being stuck in Francie Deerborne's head this morning.

Her "Voices" gripe and grumble as she tap-tap-taps her unlit cigarette on the breakfast table, observing Iris who sits across from her. And she does *not* like what she sees.

Who does that filthy bed-wetter think she is, sittin' there like a queen presiding over her Cream of Wheat?

Francie is especially annoyed by Iris's bold calm, considering she found the girl's nightgown, soaking wet, hid in the trough behind the chicken coop. Francie thinks Iris must've washed it out because it didn't stink of urine, but she was not fooled one bit!

And now here Iris sits, ramrod straight, eating her cereal like she has all the time in the world. A dunce's smile on her simple face!

Francie would like to tell Iris a thing or two about what it's like to be the mother of a child neighbors think is as strange and pitiful as a three-legged dog.

Yep, Francie's one spark away from a prairie fire, but she keeps her yap shut because Hank's eating with them. Shoving a sopping piece of toast through his fried eggs, runny and disgusting just the way he likes them.

If Francie says one thin word against his "Bird," Hank might lock up the liquor cabinet and throw away the key. She wouldn't put it past him.

Francie's thoughts are shattered by two blaring car horn honks from outside.

"Who on God's green earth is making all that racket?" Francie exclaims. She turns back to Iris. "Well, go on and look young lady, 'stead of sitting there like a wall-eyed dunce."

Iris rushes to do her mother's bidding. What she sees through the kitchen window makes her gasp with gladness.

"Who is it?" Francie presses.

"It's Maggie!"

"Who's Maggie?"

Iris turns and looks her mother square in the eye. "She's my friend."

Then the child snatches up her books and is out the door before Francie can clamp her jaw shut. And Hank, God bless him, looks like a man who just won a prize.

~ ~ ~ ~ ~

Maggie's about to lay on the horn again when Iris dashes through the screen door and hurries toward her, books glued to her chest, as is her habit.

Maggie leans across the bench seat and pushes open the passenger door. Iris hops in, face shining. "Thanks for taking me to school!"

"Don't thank me yet," Maggie says, throwing the car into reverse. "'Cuz we're ditching!"

~ ~ ~ ~ ~

Maggie's Packard flies through flat country, windows rolled down, the radio blasting that hip-swiveling God, Elvis Presley's "That's Alright Mama."

The wind whips the girls' hair around their heads like gold-and-chestnut streamers as they burn rubber.

Suddenly WaKeeney's claustrophobic fields become wide open spaces. The girls have got just one pitstop before embarking on their adventure.

90

~ ~ ~ ~ ~

Chewing a fingernail, Iris perches on the edge of a neatly tucked, sky-blue chenille spread topping the Richmonds' king-sized marital bed.

Lacy curtains billow through an open window, and sun glints off the silver-capped perfume bottles on Grace's walnut dresser.

While Iris hovers, Maggie ransacks her mother's closet, tossing lavender-scented sweaters and skirts to the bedroom floor along with an ocean of heels.

"Are you sure your mom won't come back and catch us?" Iris asks nervously.

"I could read *The Odyssey* faster than Grace Richmond shops for shoes."

"Your mom sure does have a lot of them," Iris says, wonderingly.

"She likes to accessorize her natural glamour," Maggie snorts. "Aha! Here's something!" Maggie brandishes a wine-colored sweater twinset on a hanger. "Try this on!"

Iris balks, smoothing her own sensible navy skirt. "Oh, no. I don't think that's a good idea."

Maggie thrusts it at her. "You said you wished to be like me for one day. It starts right here with Grace's twinset, which she'll hand down to me in a year, whether I want it or not. I have to admit her sweaters look real chic with a felt pencil skirt, though Grace'd prefer I wear them with a poodle skirt to give me hips."

Iris eyes the clothes with deep mistrust. Not to be put off, Maggie shakes the sweater in front of Iris's face.

Reluctantly, Iris extends her hand.

~ ~ ~ ~ ~

Maggie paces impatiently in front of the barricaded master bathroom door. "Iris, come on out and show me." Silence. "Iris?"

"Yes?" a muffled response from behind the bathroom door.

"Come out here and lemme see how you look."

"No."

"Come on now, I wanna see."

"You mom's clothes are too tight."

"Lemme see."

A long silence, thick with internal deliberation, follows. Then Iris, eyes down, cheeks red, shuffles out of the master bath squeezed into Grace's sweater set.

"I'm too big to wear your mom's stuff," she says as she plucks the clinging material away from her bust.

Maggie gazes with approval. "Iris, that's how it's s'posed to look."

"I don't think so."

"I'm tellin' you, it is."

"I feel too … too …" she flounders. "Look-at-able!"

Maggie laughs. "That's not a word."

"It should be," Iris fusses. "When I said I wanted to be you for one day, I didn't mean I want to *look* like you. I could never be that chic. I meant I don't want to take any guff like you. That I want to be strong … and, I guess, confident like you."

Maggie nods, thinking. "Well, sometimes lookin' good is like wearin' armor that makes you feel more confident. It's a work-from-the-outside-in sorta thing. Now try these on!" Maggie holds out a towering pair of spectator heels.

Iris gasps. "I'll break my fool neck in those things!"

"That's the price you pay for confidence, Iris. The open-and-shut price of confidence.

~ ~ ~ ~ ~

After squeezing in and out of an endless parade of Grace Richmond's fripperies — scarlet, royal blue and coral, which Maggie called "jewel-tones" — Iris settles on a violet crop-cardigan that complements her eyes and a circle skirt that doesn't make her bottom look like what her Grandpa Ferdie would call, "two pitbulls fighting in a gunny sack."

"Okay, now for phase two of becoming me!" Maggie dangles a money clip full of bills in front of Iris's face.

"Where'd you get that?"

"Grace is always slipping me money after my dad loses his temper. It makes her feel less guilty, I guess."

Maggie jams the money clip into her purse. "Spending it on you'll make me feel less guilty for taking it."

~ ~ ~ ~ ~

Before Iris knows the train has left the station, Maggie plants her on a stool at the Woolworth's beauty counter.

Wearing a helmet of tight curls, a face lacquered to within an inch of its life and a nameplate that reads, "Miss Juniper Trimbley," a formidable middle-aged beautician appraises the girls shrewdly from behind her cat-eye glasses.

"Hi there," Maggie greets her. "I've brought my friend Iris in for a beauty make-over."

"She thinks she's my fairy godmother," Iris grumbles.

"I see," Miss Trimbley murmurs.

The beautician sets about inspecting all angles of Iris's face, calculating the potential of her obscured eyes and nerve-bitten lips.

It'll be a task to bring this girl up to snuff, but Miss Trimbley considers herself the Michelangelo of face paint and feels up to the challenge.

"With your fair complexion, an apricot or a peach palette would suit you best," the beautician reports. "We'll start with Elizabeth Arden's 'Honey Bee Pressed Powder'."

Iris looks doubtful. "Maggie, I don't think this'll work. Mama says I look like a carnival clown with makeup on my face."

Maggie bolsters Iris like a corner man pep-talking his boxer. "She's just jealous 'cuz you're young and she's not."

"She's beautiful and I'm not."

Maggie huffs. "Beauty's in the eye of the beholder and I'd lay odds Mrs. Deerborne wouldn't impress me. Now stop yappin' or Miss Trimbley'll make a mess."

"Don't worry about me," the beautician assures Maggie, laying out her arsenal of brushes. "I can put a full face on whilst driving over the Jepson train tracks without smearing. I was trained in Shawnee at the Max Factor Academy."

"Impressive," Maggie fights a smile.

"You have no idea, young lady," Miss Trimbley asserts.

Over the better part of an hour, Iris squirms under an onslaught of applicators, cotton balls and sponges. Miss Trimbley is evidently no amateur when it comes to working with rough clay.

"Do I really need these?" Iris asks Miss Trimbley, who is in the process of gluing false eyelashes on her subject. "It feels like two bats have landed on my eyes!"

"There are certain sacrifices we must make to achieve our glamour potential," the beautician responds firmly.

"I've been tellin' Iris, puttin' our best foot forward boosts confidence," Maggie chimes in.

"Oh, abtholutely," Miss Trimbley lisps around an eye pencil clamped between her teeth. "The right shade of red lipsthick can shoot a lady's confidenth through the roof, which ith why we finith with a bold lip."

The beautician returns the eye pencil smartly to the appropriate pocket in her make-up apron and retrieves a small lipstick tube.

"This one's called 'Sunset Passion'," she says, presenting the lipstick like it was a rare bottle of wine.

A moment of whimsy overtakes Miss Trimbley. "I imagine wearing it after being shipwrecked on a deserted island with Vic Damone."

Moments later, the beautician steps back to admire her work. She can't help brimming with pride at her masterpiece. "Jane Russell, eat your heart out!"

"Would you look at that?" Maggie breathes. "All Iris's face needed was a little definition!"

"Let me see," Iris murmurs, putting her glasses back on.

Maggie stops her. "Not yet!" she cries, "You look like a doll, but let's leave these off for now."

Iris squawks as Maggie seizes the horn-rimmed hunk off of her nose. "You have to put those back on. I'm legally blind!"

"Then you won't get arrested." Maggie spins Iris's chair toward the mirror. "Go ahead and look."

Iris squints. "Honestly Maggie, I can't see anything but a red blotch."

"Fine. Here." Maggie hands Iris her glasses back, sighing. Iris puts them on and gazes into the mirror again. She feels water pressing hard against the back of her eyes.

"Don't you dare cry," Miss Trimbley shouts. "You'll ruin the entire effect!"

"But. That's not me," Iris whispers.

The makeup indeed defines Iris's soft features, giving shape to her dark brows, adding cheekbones and framing her light blue eyes.

Iris can't help staring, turning this way and that, as if to assure herself the image isn't just a picture on the wall.

"Now," Maggie coaxes, "sell lips." Maggie forms her lips into an "O" and blows while Iris looks on.

"Maggie?" Iris interrupts.

"Yes?"

"You look like a bottom-feeding, red-gill grouper in the Smokey Hill River when you do that."

Ignoring Iris, Maggie slaps Grace's guilt money on the counter and tells Miss Trimbley, "We'll take everything you put on her face. All of it!"

"I'd suggest nothing less," the beautician nods as she rings them up.

~ ~ ~ ~ ~

Jeff pulls his motorbike up in front of Aunt Pat's Diner where he plans to order Wednesday's chicken potpie lunch special.

Of course, most WaKeeney High seniors prefer to brown-bag it with their crowd, even though they're allowed to leave campus. But Jeff takes every opportunity to make tracks out of school. It's not because, as a farmer, he won't need Shakespeare and *The Art of the Narrative Essay*. It's that Jeff's entirely detached from kids his age.

At seventeen he feels seventy, while his classmates, gossiping around a lunch table, seem to exist in some parallel universe reserved for the untested. Jeff hasn't felt like a child since my exit from this mortal coil.

As he lowers his kickstand outside Aunt Pat's, he spots the new girl, Maggie Richmond, promenading down Marlborough Avenue with a girl he doesn't recognize.

Pretty much every guy's tongue lolls out whenever Maggie walks by and Jeff can't blame them. She's a sight to behold, with those thick-lashed eyes and that whippet waist.

Maggie and her friend stop to peer at dresses in the display window of Lula Mae's Bridal and Dance Shop.

Jeff puzzles over the second girl. The shape of her head is familiar. The roundness of her shoulders. But he just can't place her. Until she turns her face his way. That's when he sees the glasses. It's Iris, but it's not.

She's dressed different … like other girls. In a sweater and a skirt that make her look like … well … like a woman. Jeff frowns a little, not sure he likes it. But there is one change in Iris that makes his heart glad.

She's linked arms with Maggie and she's smiling. Smiling! The same girl he last saw sobbing and running from an upturned basket of broken eggs.

For a moment, he starts toward her, as if to introduce himself to this freshly blooming Iris. But as he watches the girls and hears their light chatter, Jeff pulls aside instead and heads into the diner for Aunt Pat's perfect pie.

He's a gentleman, that one. He knows when to shut the drawing-room door and let the ladies be.

~ ~ ~ ~ ~

"Oh, Iris, look at that little darling," Maggie exclaims,

pointing at a champagne satin dress draped becomingly on a mannequin in Lula Mae's window.

Iris gazes at the dress with hungry eyes. "It's so elegant."

Maggie watches her friend, then makes a decision. "Come on," she says, pulling Iris to the door.

Iris snaps out of her reverie. "What?"

"You're goin' to try it on."

"Why?"

"Just for fun."

Iris balks. "But, I don't have anywhere to wear that. It makes no sense."

"Sometimes, Iris, things don't hafta make sense."

"But …"

"No buts!" Maggie's reveling in her power. "Remember, you're 'me' for today and I get to tell 'me' what to do!"

Iris has been told what to do every single day of her life. But for the first time, it's fun.

~ ~ ~ ~ ~

On a dais in front of a three-way mirror, Iris beholds herself swathed in the dress from the display window.

Folds of lush satin brush the floor at Iris's feet. The empire waist gathers just below the bust at Iris's narrowest place and the wide neckline shows off her womanly curves — still somewhat to her horror.

Far off in the universe, the memory of Francie's Pepto-Bismol horror bursts like an imploding planet.

"I hardly recognize myself," Iris murmurs, uncertain.

"It's meant for you," Maggie says simply.

Iris considers that possibility. She turns suddenly. "I can't let you spend your mom's money on this."

"Of course you can!"

Iris shakes her head. "It wouldn't be right." She can't believe she's considering what she's considering. It feels so rash! But maybe 'rash' is good?

"I been savin' my egg money for new saddlebacks," Iris tells Maggie. "I guess … I could spend it on this and put the rest on layaway."

She brings the silky fabric of the hem up to caress her face.

That's when reality strikes.

Before Iris's very eyes, the fabric darkens and goes dripping wet in her hands. She drops the hem like it's contaminated.

But the dress is soiled only in Iris's mind. Even so, she meets Maggie's eyes in the mirror.

"I'd just ruin it," she says. "That's why Mama never buys me anything nice."

Maggie mightily wishes Francie Deerborne would materialize from thin air so she could sock her in the jaw. But she gets a better idea.

"I know where we're going next," Maggie declares.

The rebellious set of her fiery friend's jaw worries Iris.

~ ~ ~ ~ ~

Iris fidgets in a crowded doctor's office with Maggie, listening to the clock *clack-clack-clack-clack* the long minutes away like a demented woodpecker.

Makeup is one thing. Dress-shopping another. But seeing a doctor about her Terrible Shame has Iris dying to float off the waiting room chair, through the ceiling, and into a world where no one's ever heard her name.

"Let's go," Iris pleads to Maggie. "We'll get caught."

"No, we won't," Maggie vows.

"Somehow, some way Mama will find out." Iris pleads. "She finds out *everything*."

"This time she won't," Maggie says, determined.

Just then, a Nurse Whipple sticks her head into the waiting room, wearing her starched nurse's cap like a pith helmet and surveying the patient roster as if it were a military roll call.

"Iris Deerborne?" the nurse barks.

"Jump down Jesus," Maggie mutters as she and Iris stand, "This one got her corporal stripes in Korea."

Nurse Whipple cocks a brow as Maggie tries to join Iris. "Patients only."

"I'm Iris's sister, Margot, and my folks said I have to keep an eye on her."

Nurse Whipple stares hard. She'll acquiesce but there are rules. "You'll have to wait in the hallway. Quietly. Do *not* disturb any patients under any circumstance. Do you have Avian flu?"

"I try to stay away from birds. So ..."

"If I hear you cough, there will be trouble."

"Duly noted," Maggie concedes.

Not fully satisfied with the interaction, Nurse Whipple nonetheless leads both girls into a sterile white hallway punctuated by exam rooms. She stops next to the women's restroom and turns to Iris, brandishing a small medical cup.

"Go in there. Urinate in this. Then leave it in the lab. Here's a pen and there's a label on the cup where you can write your name, right here." Nurse Whipple pokes the pen at Iris.

"After that, go to exam room seven and wait, *without complaint,* for Doctor Kay. He's got too many patients and too little time!" Nurse Whipple complains, like it's Iris's fault.

Iris takes the cup and pen. Swallowing hard, she whispers to Maggie, "This is probably the first time in my life I don't think I'll be able to pee."

~ ~ ~ ~ ~

Maggie perches on a chair in the hallway outside the lab, foot jiggling a mile a minute. She reads and rereads a chart on the wall that describes all the symptoms of shell shock.

"Anxiety. Panic attacks. Outsized fears. Complete mental breakdown. Anxiety. Panic attacks. Outsized fears. Complete mental breakdown."

A door opens and an elderly, bespectacled doctor emerges from the lab carrying a medical chart.

"Doctor Kay?" Maggie asks as she rises.

He turns. "Yes, dear?"

"Do you have Iris Deerborne's results yet?"

"I do."

"I'm her sister Margot. Could you please tell me what's wrong with her?"

Doctor Kay fixes Maggie with a knowing look. "Hank Deerborne's only got one child so far's I know."

Maggie's eyes appeal to him. "Well ... I'm her friend."

Doctor Kay shrugs. "As I told her mother when she brought Iris in, many moons ago, I didn't find anything wrong with the girl."

"What d'you mean? How come she keeps wettin' herself?"

Doctor Kay taps his temple with his pen. "It's all up here. Psychosomatic."

Maggie looks defeated for a moment. Then her face blossoms with an idea.

"Doctor Kay …?" she asks, before he can disappear into exam room eight. He turns. "Maybe this time there *is* somethin' wrong with Iris?" she suggests.

Doctor Kay's about to set Maggie straight when he sees the compassion in her eyes — a medicine, in his experience, that can go a long way toward remedying something "psychosomatic."

Nodding, he pulls out his prescription pad and begins to write.

~ ~ ~ ~ ~

Young pharmacist Eddie Wilson puts a bottle of bright orange pills on the counter in front of Maggie and rings it up. "That'll be fifty-eight cents for a month's supply."

Iris hides behind a display rack of Gillette lady razors, praying Eddie doesn't know that the pills with her name on them are for a bladder condition. He's as handsome as a fireman and smart as Mac McGarry, the host of Iris's favorite quiz show, *It's Academic*.

Maggie puts down two quarters, a nickel and three pennies, then rubbernecks for Iris. She spots her protégé reading the label on an after-shave kit as if it were written in Holy Sanskrit.

Maggie marches over and hands Iris the bottle. "Doctor Kay says one tablet twice a day should do the trick."

"That's it?" Iris asks, incredulous.

"That's it. He says they work on the metabolic system, which informs the bladder."

Iris squints Maggie down, knowing her friend's penchant for lying and exaggeration.

"Didn't he tell you that?" Maggie asks, wide-eyed as a lamb.

"He said they'd help, but Mama says, 'once a bed wetter, always a bed wetter.'"

Maggie snorts. "Your mama doesn't know her ass from her elbow."

"Maggie, all this change is just too much!"

"Then take it one step at a time. And the next step is taking one of these pills."

Iris reaches for them. "I'm gonna be like normal people?"

"Good God, I hope not," Maggie says. "Normal people mostly let me down."

~ ~ ~ ~ ~

Twenty minutes later, Maggie and Iris roar up to Hazel Atkins's Beauty Salon, both girls belting "Hello Mary Lou" along with the dreamy Ricky Nelson on the radio.

(Those lips. Those eyes!)

But as Maggie parks, Iris spots an evil portent in Hazel's driveway. It bursts the magical bubble she and Maggie have created outside the WaKeeney pecking order.

"That's Clarissa Dell's car," Iris says dully, pointing to a '57 Chevy sedan.

"Oh."

The girls sit quietly a moment. "We can come back another time," Iris offers.

"Okay." Maggie turns the key in the ignition, sparking the engine back to life. As she adjusts the rearview mirror, Maggie accidentally catches sight of her own eyes. She doesn't like what she sees.

Taking a deep breath, Maggie turns the engine off and pulls the keys out of the ignition. She looks at Iris. Iris looks back, stiff as an Indian totem.

"No," Iris pleads.

"Yes."

"They'll kick you out of Songbirds."

"Let 'em try."

"You don't have to do this."

"Yes, I do."

"Why?"

"Because to hell with them."

"Well, I don't want to go in," Iris declares.

"Do I have to remind you that today you don't take any guff?"

Iris says nothing, her mouth a thin line.

Maggie presses. "Are you 'me' for today or was this all just nothing?"

Iris sighs, defeated. "I'm 'you' for today."

"Then you know I'm not the kinda girl to walk away from a fight. Now, let's go."

~ ~ ~ ~ ~

To Iris's ears, Hazel's tinkling bell echoes to the county line and back. Like a convict led to the stocks, she lets Maggie pull her further into the beauty parlor.

Immediately, Iris locks eyes with her executioner,

Clarissa, who sits under the sole dryer bell sporting tight, bitsy curlers in her hair.

Rhonda roosts nearby, her freckled hands soaking in bowls of warm water.

Hattie flips through October's *Life* magazine as her 'Fun Fuchsia' toenail polish dries.

There's a wordless moment that crackles the air. Clarissa's eyes narrow. And then, as if summoned by the gods, Hazel comes to the rescue.

"Iris Deerborne, is that you?" She crosses the room to the anxious, newly-arrived patrons like a refreshing breeze.

"Hi, Hazel," Iris croaks, her throat suddenly gone spitless. A heaviness settles in her bladder, but her new pills seem to be working!

"Look at you, all dolled up!" Hazel takes Iris's face in her hands. "You've always been lovely, but now you're drop-dead gorgeous!"

"One look at Iris and you drop dead," Clarissa mutters just loud enough for everyone to hear.

Hattie and Rhonda, who know exactly where their bread is buttered, laugh like five-cent rodeo clowns.

Iris backs toward the door. "You look busy," she tells Hazel.

"Not at all. Clarissa and Hattie are drying and Rhonda needs to soak."

Rhonda lifts her fingers from the water. "I've already been soaking ten minutes! I'm turning into a prune!"

"You have some rough callouses, dear," Hazel notes.

"We've gotta get Iris ready for the School Spirit After-Game dance," Maggie announces.

This news shocks the Songbirds to their bobby socks. "But Iris never goes to dances!" Rhonda declares, like it's law.

"Not a one," Hattie agrees.

"That's right, I don't," Iris confirms.

"Well, *I* do," Maggie tells Iris, "So you will too."

"I think that's a wonderful idea," Hazel interjects.

Under the hair dryer, Clarissa rolls her eyes. "What would a dance be without a wallflower?" The room falls silent. Clarissa smiles. "Just kidding, of course."

"You know, Clarissa," Hazel says, all business, "I don't think I put enough permanent solution in your hair. I'll be right there as soon as I figure out what to do with all of Iris's *natural* curl."

As Hazel ushers Iris to a chair, Maggie saunters over to the Songbirds, finds a stool and plops down as if she didn't just flout their orders.

"What're you doin'?" Clarissa hisses. "Didn't we tell you Iris is an Untouchable?"

"You did," Maggie says coolly. "But my dad doesn't see it that way."

"What're you talkin' about?" Clarissa sputters.

"I know this sounds crazy," Maggie says, examining her nails, "but he's photographing Iris for the magazine."

"For *Life* magazine?" gasps Hattie, looking amazed to find an edition of that very publication in her hand.

Maggie nods. "Somehow he got this idea he had to find the 'Heart of the Heartland' for his next piece. He thinks Iris is deep ... as deep and far-reaching as the plains of Kansas."

The three Songbirds' heads swivel as one to gape at Iris,

trying mightily to see her "depth."

Iris has ditched her glasses in preparation for a hair wash. She squints at herself in the mirror, just trying to *see*, period.

Clarissa sniffs. "The 'Heart of the Heartland'? More like 'Mister Magoo of Mulvane'."

"Maybe we know Iris too well to really see her?" ruminates Hattie.

"I think I see it. Her depth," Rhonda murmurs.

"Iris may or may not be the 'Heart of the Heartland,'" Clarissa sneers, turning to her betrayers, "but one thing I know for sure is the two of you are about as smart as bait!"

She shoves up the dryer bell and turns her full indignity upon the hairdresser. "Hazel," she snaps. "I insist you take these rollers out before I end up looking like Little Orphan Annie!"

~ ~ ~ ~ ~

Half an hour later, the coast is clear. Clarissa, Rhonda and Hattie have skedaddled, taking the tension in the room with them.

Maggie, Iris and Hazel have eased into a comfortable silence as Hazel *snip, snip, snips* away at Iris's bushy mane. Finally, she steps back with a smile.

"My magnum opus is complete."

Hazel spins Iris around, presenting her to Maggie. Hazel has trimmed and smoothed Iris's hair into a modern, flattering bob. An egg-sized lump forms in Maggie's throat.

"What is it?" Iris worries. "What's wrong?"

"Nothing's wrong! You look ..." she swallows hard and smiles. "… just perfect."

Iris grabs her glasses from the shelf by the mirror and

puts them on. As she looks, her mouth falls open like an oven door. "Seems like I can't hardly recognize myself today."

"That's you, honey," Hazel assures her, squeezing Iris's shoulders. Then Hazel turns to Maggie.

"Now, what about you, sweetheart?" she asks, pocketing her scissors. "Why don't you take a seat so I can work out what to do with your glorious head of hair. We could figure out a look for prom."

Maggie concedes. "Sure. Why not?"

Iris gratefully bounces up so Maggie can take the focus off of her. Nice as it's been, being the center of attention is exhausting. She darts around Hazel's shop picking up floral-smelling ointments, sneezy talcums, curling wands and tweezer sets.

Moving past Hazel's shampoo display, Iris comes upon a framed photograph of a skinny, spotty, kind-faced young man in a soldier's uniform.

"Who's this, Hazel?" Iris asks, picking up the photo.

Hazel glances up. When she sees what Iris is holding she smiles fondly, though there's a shadow in that smile.

"That's a boy I loved." Hazel says simply. "He died in the Korean War."

"I'm so sorry," Iris murmurs. "I didn't know."

"Oh no, don't be sorry. I never talk about him." Quietly, Hazel resumes her work.

"I didn't mean to be nosy," Iris apologizes.

Hazel turns back, looking patient. "I don't mind talkin' about him with you, Iris. I guess you hate town gossip just as much as I do."

"That's the truth."

"His name was Glen, and he was about the gentlest person I've ever known …" Her eyes soften. "I don't understand how God can let the good ones die so young."

Just then, Hazel brushes Maggie's hair away from her face, accidentally revealing the deep purple bruise Gerald's belt left above Maggie's right cheekbone. Hazel touches it lightly, causing Maggie to flinch and grab Hazel's hand.

Their eyes meet in the mirror. Something passes between them. They both know the significance of the bruise, understanding it in the same way.

Abruptly, Maggie stands. "I don't really know how I want my hair for prom, yet. It depends on the dress."

"Of course," Hazel replies, wiping her hands on her apron, careful not to meet Maggie's eye. "The dress always picks the hair. You come back once you find it."

Maggie grabs Iris by the sleeve. "Let's vamoose, kid."

"Okay. Thanks, Hazel," Iris says.

"You're welcome, sweetheart."

Through the parlor window, Hazel watches Maggie and Iris drive off in a whirl of dust. She keeps staring long after Maggie's car has disappeared.

Finally, Hazel walks over and picks up the framed picture, studying the soldier's serious, young face. "Where are you when I need you?" she whispers.

Chapter Six

I'll say *this* much for Francie: normally she doesn't drink before supper. She thinks people who drink early have a "problem with the sauce" and Francie does *not* have a "problem with the sauce."

But today, she's three-sheets-to-the-wind on Old Crow and it's barely four o'clock in the afternoon.

She blames the postman, Jim Dawson, for her current condition. Francie had just done a load of washing when Jim came to her door, the goiter in his neck looking larger and nastier than ever. But she could abide looking at the thing long enough to snatch the *Sears* catalogue out of his hands.

Francie with a *Sears* catalogue is like a dog with a pound of raw meat. She can't resist it, but she sure as shootin' can't handle it, either.

Holed up on the sofa in the family room, Francie flipped through pages of models — no damn prettier than she is — garbed in pure silk Shantungs, classic Brentshire shirtwaists, pink scalloped necklines, swing and pencil skirts, gloves and pillbox hats.

Usually the models stand before plain white backdrops with one manicured hand on a hip and the other resting flat on top of a thigh. Today's catalogue, though, was special. It was the "Urbane" edition.

Inside its pages, the mannequins galloped across intersections in busy New York City and sipped tea with pointed pinkies at The Cosmopolitan Hotel.

And handsome men — whose polished shoes had never once stepped on hardpan — escorted the ladies to the

Metropolitan Opera at the Lincoln Center and to eat Lobster Newburg at Saks Fifth Avenue.

Francie's personal New York City experience had been a little different, thank you very much. She and Rusty Allred lived a year in an Irish tenement flat in Hell's Kitchen.

Rusty spent most his time there drinking Jim Beam Kentucky straight, losing at Hearts to knee-capping thugs, and whoring around with whatever money Francie brought in slinging eggs and hash browns at Joe's Diner on 45th and Eighth Avenue.

The closest Francie ever got to the Metropolitan Opera was buying a bag of chestnuts from a cart vendor across the street.

No wonder Francie decided to invite Old Crow to this pity party.

Trouble is the scotch hasn't really helped. While those damn models were primping for a night at El Morocco, Francie had nothing to look forward to but folding the yellowed boxer shorts of a man who preferred the company of Guernsey cows and Berkshire swine to hers.

By the time Francie was well and properly schnockered, she'd torn the *Sears* catalogue into a million angry little pieces.

With one giant flap of her skirt, Francie blasted the shreds away from her like a confetti cannon.

They floated in the air, sifting into the cracks and crevices in the family room club chairs, the fringe of the fake Persian rug, the strands of Francie's matted hair.

Even now, a few wayward bits find their way inside Francie's Maidenform brassiere, nestling there as Francie falls back on the couch and her eyes blink, blink, blink closed.

~ ~ ~ ~ ~

As the clocks strikes five in WaKeeney, Iris sneaks into the farmhouse through the backdoor hoping to evade her mother who could knock the wind out of this nearly perfect day.

She's just about to slip up the staircase to her bedroom undetected when, out of the corner of her eye, she spots the very person she's trying to avoid.

Francie lies splayed out on the couch in the family room, dead to the world.

Iris spots one empty liquor bottle shattered on the tiled fireplace apron and a second one, half empty, lying on its side, drip-drip-dripping onto the coffee table.

Iris sees cigarette butts choking an ashtray. Shreds of paper from a now-unidentifiable source infesting everything. And Francie cradling an empty tumbler to her chest like a child's blankie.

The sight — and smell — tell Iris that her mama won't be waking any time soon.

But before Iris heads upstairs, she looks again. This time she takes in Francie's worn cotton robe, the smattering of gray hairs at her temples, the helpless face smeared with attempts to recapture waning youth.

During this appraisal, something unexpected happens. For once Iris doesn't see this woman with fear, disgust, or even pity — though God knows all three are justified. Instead of "Mama," Iris sees "Francie."

Mama's the person who makes every day a living hell. But Francie is a person separate from Iris. A person Iris realizes must be unhappy. Maybe even as unhappy as Iris is?

Decided, Iris makes an about-face, slips into the family room and sets to tidying up.

She retrieves and sweeps up the bottles, dumping them out back. She empties and wipes the ashtray clean. Sweeps up the scattered bits of paper, picking some of them out of the carpet one by one on hands and knees.

Before leaving, Iris retrieves the crocheted blanket draped across the back of the couch and settles it over her mother.

~ ~ ~ ~ ~

That night, just an hour and eight minutes before the School Spirit After-Game dance, Clarissa fumes at her vanity table.

Apparently Hazel Atkins *did* leave those tiny permanent curlers in her hair too damned long and now — just like she feared — Clarissa looks like Little Orphan Annie with a head full of corkscrews!

"That *woman!*" she sputters, flinging down her useless comb. "I'll put a dent in her business if it's the *last* thing I do, so help me God!"

A few houses down, Rhonda Robertson is also none too happy standing in front of her own bathroom mirror. A whole new corona of pimples march across her forehead. These lousy zits are ruining her life!

Across town, Hattie's having the darndest time getting her darling new circle skirt to zip up!

To her left is her mirror. To her right, a fresh bag of chips. She do-si-dos between them, looking longingly at one and miserably at the other.

How is it Clarissa can eat six pounds of french fries and lose weight, while Hattie gains five pounds if she just takes a deep breath? It isn't fair!

Meanwhile, Iris sits at her own vanity dressed in Grace Richmond's pink angora sweater, deep turquoise swing skirt and — at Maggie's insistence — a pair of tan-and-white spectator pumps with three-inch heels.

For a moment, she gapes at the "girl" in the mirror. A stranger. An imposter. A not-Iris.

"One step at a time," she tells the mirror. "That's what Maggie says."

She reaches for the bag of new makeup. Concentrating, she methodically applies one product at a time. Foundation. Rouge. Powder. Mascara. She finishes with the bold red "Sunset Passion" lipstick.

For a fleeting moment, Iris "sells lips" in the mirror.

~ ~ ~ ~ ~

At their kitchen table, Hank watches a haggard Francie push ham hocks and beans around on her plate to make it look like she's eaten some.

An hour earlier, after hosing down the barn and getting the cows back into their feedlots, Hank had discovered Francie sitting on the couch in the family room, green at the gills and a muddled look on her face.

He beelined to the outdoor garbage and found exactly what he knew would be there: two too many nut-colored bottles.

Marching inside, Hank informed Francie he'd cook dinner tonight. Then he rustled up those ham hocks and beans — the meal Francie puked up after her last bender.

Hank was too smart to launch a direct offensive against

Francie's liquor. That tactic only made things worse.

He knew his wife would take off hell-bent-for-leather in the '45 Desoto hard-top Hank got her when she came back from New York.

Time and again, she'd drive through the night to find a hooch house in a far off town while Hank laid awake all night, stomach in knots, waiting for Francie to come home.

Sometimes she'd return, still defiant, and climb in bed, turning her back on him for days, even weeks to come.

Other times, she'd come home repentant, taking Hank by the wrist and leading him to bed, taking his clothes off piece by piece, and making him feel the deep, dark pleasure that sank him all over again.

Worse than Francie's return were the hours she was gone. Hank would listen for a knock on the door from state police, there to tell him his wife had finally wrapped her car around an electrical pole at the intersection of Interstate 70 and U.S. Route 283. That she'd crossed over to the Great Beyond, forever out of reach.

Better to fight against his mortal enemy — the liquid poison — by punishing her with a meal that would bring it up and out.

Francie glares at Hank across the kitchen table. She knows exactly what he's up to and she'll be damned if she lets him get the better of her. Pride and anger make her force a spoonful of the gelatinous ham hock into her mouth.

This is when Iris appears. Hank's fork freezes midair, his wife forgotten.

In that moment, I see exactly what Hank sees. A young woman — hair tamed, makeup in place, wearing new finery — who is the spitting image of Hank's Mama, Marti, when she was crowned Harvest Queen of 1923.

Hank puts down his fork. "Who is this angel before me?" he asks, causing Iris to blush with pleasure.

Francie, struck dumb, gulps down the bit of slimy ham hock.

"Maggie gave me a beauty makeover," Iris tells her father.

"You're always my beautiful Bird," Hank declares, "But tonight you're a beautiful young lady."

"Thanks, Daddy," she says softly.

Iris looks hopefully at Francie, whose eyes roam over her daughter high and low. "What d'you think, Mama?"

The question breaks Francie from a trance.

"I think I'd like to know where you got the money for that get-up? We don't have that kinda money just lyin' round the house, you know."

Hank turns on her. "It's all right if Iris spent a little allowance on herself!"

"And where're your glasses?" Francie grills her daughter.

Iris tries for a brave response. "I took 'em off … just for tonight. I'm goin' to the school dance."

"You're not goin' anywhere without those glasses. Now, you head right back upstairs and put 'em on!"

"I'll be careful, Mama."

Hank pounds the table. "Francie, for once in your life could you lay off of Iris? What harm is there? What harm if she's happy?"

"Don't you be tellin' me how to mind my child," Francie says, warming to the battle. "Edith says this Maggie girl's mom drives a brand spanking new Cadillac and gets her clothes from Dior. With fancy folks like that, what's gonna happen when this Maggie decides she doesn't like the way Iris smells?"

"But Mama, see, Maggie helped me with that too ..." Iris begins.

Francie interrupts, staring right into her daughter's eyes. "Girl like that probably likes spendin' time with a plain girl so she can feel even better 'bout herself."

Francie's dagger hits its mark. Iris deflates before all our eyes.

"Francie, leave her be, now I mean it!" shouts Hank. "You're like a cat eatin' her own young! I won't stand for it, woman. I won't stand for it anymore!"

"Isn't that just like the two of you, gangin' up on me," Francie cries. "It's always the two of you against me! It's a wonder you even let me live in my own house!"

Francie shoves her chair back, totters to her feet and exits the room with a theatricality rivaling anything on the Great White Way.

Hank stands up hard, panting like a winded runner. He walks over to Iris and pulls her into an awkward, but warm embrace, tenderly stroking her hair.

"Honey, your mama loves you. She does. She just ..." he flounders. "She just don't know how to show it."

Hank releases Iris, looks into her eyes, willing his daughter to persevere.

"You go on now. You go on to that dance. Go on and enjoy yourself."

As if on cue, the sound of glass breaking issues from the upstairs master bedroom. It's followed by a much louder crash.

Hank sighs. "I better check on her." And he moves

toward the door.

Iris stands where her daddy left her, as if incapable of locomotion.

Hank turns back. "You go on to that dance. It's no crime to be happy. You deserve to be happy, sweetheart."

Then he's gone.

~ ~ ~ ~ ~

Maggie pulls up outside the Deerborne farmhouse with a squeal of tires and lays on the horn. She's more excited to bring Iris to the dance than she is to go herself.

But Iris doesn't appear, Maggie hops out of her car and bounds up the Deerborne's porch steps, knocking on the front door to beat the band.

Just as Maggie raises a fist to knock again, the front door opens a crack. Iris peers through the narrow slit. Wet, black mascara runs down the girl's face. Her thick glasses obscure her eyes.

Maggie starts. "Iris, what's goin' on? What happened to your make-up?"

"Nothin'."

"Lemme in and I'll help you fix it. But we gotta move fast or we're gonna be late."

Iris doesn't look up. "I'm not going to the dance."

"What d'you mean you're not going?"

She won't meet Maggie's eye. "I just don't want to go."

"Is it your mother? Where is she? I wanna talk to that woman!"

"That's not it. I just don't want to go, I said!"

"I know it's that mother of yours," Maggie spits, now

sparking mad. "And I'm not gonna let her get away with it!"

"Maggie, I can't go," Iris pleads.

"Why not? Why can't you go?"

Iris shrugs. "Because it don't matter if I have different hair, or different clothes, or a different face ... I'm still me. I'm still the same girl I always was." Her voice drops, "I'm still an Untouchable."

Maggie presses the door open wider. "Not to me you're not," she declares. "To me you're better than all of the people in this town combined."

The words drop like stones at Iris's feet, meaning nothing.

"I'm sorry, Maggie. I made up my mind," Iris says then pulls back and gently closes the door in Maggie's face.

Maggie stands there a moment, like a lost boat on a windless sea. Then she turns and walks slowly back to her car, gets inside and slams the door shut. After several long minutes, Maggie turns the key in the ignition.

She'd like nothing better than to skip the dance now. But she has to go for the exact same reason Iris won't. To tread a path influenced by her parents.

~ ~ ~ ~ ~

This year the WaKeeney High party planning committee did a bang up job with the After-Game dance decorations.

Red-and-blue pennants and streamers hang on every inch of the gymnasium and a huge banner over the entrance reads, "Panthers, Panthers, Go Fight Win!!"

Spit-shined boys and girls filter inside the gym, sending up a wall of raucous chatter and laughter.

Girls cluster in groups, eyeing boys who loiter in the

shadows, trying to look too cool to dance.

Vexed teachers patrol the perimeter on the lookout for sweaty, roaming hands.

As Bobby Darin croons "Dream Lover" over the PA, Maggie walks through the entrance of the gym under a canopy of balloons and colored lights.

In a moment, she spots the Songbirds huddled by the refreshments table where football players are known to linger in the hopes of spiking the punch bowl.

Rhonda catches Maggie's eye. "There she is!" Rhonda shrieks, "Maggie, here, here! Over here!"

Chin up, Maggie weaves through the dancers to the Songbird group. Amid the full-skirted florals and peachy twinsets, Maggie startles by contrast. She wears a simple black sheath and black kitten heels. She's one of those rare creatures that needs nothing but a simple frame to showcase her beauty.

"Good God, Rhonda," Clarissa hisses. "Pipe down! Maggie looks like a mortician in that get-up and you're actin' like she's Jesus risen."

But Rhonda can't contain herself. "You made the squad!" she shrieks at Maggie.

"You're officially a Songbird!" Hattie whoops, grabbing Maggie around the neck.

"Which means you're officially one of us," Clarissa allows.

Maggie tries to look thrilled … and fails. "Wow. That's great!" she mumbles.

Clarissa shoots an eyebrow up at Maggie's obvious lack of proper appreciation for her new exalted status. If it weren't for all the male attention this city girl draws, Clarissa wouldn't give her the time of day.

Clarissa's other brow comes up when Maggie asks her, "What happened to your hair?"

Unconsciously, Clarissa puts a hand up to the polka dot scarf currently obscuring her head and pulls it down over a few rogue curls.

"Hazel turned her into a poodle!" laughs Hattie, yanking up a corner of Clarissa's scarf to reveal the mass of tight, springy corkscrews.

Clarissa swats the hand away. "That's a lie, Hattie McCoy. It's time scarves came back into fashion and this one's a hundred percent charmeuse, bought in the Manhattan Bloomingdales when my mom was there on her honeymoon."

"Now," Clarissa changes the topic, "the first order of business for our new Songbird is to find her a prom date,"

"Brian Embrick already asked me," Hattie gloats.

"Yes, the midget asked Hattie," Clarissa confirms.

"He's not a midget!"

"His eyes are level with her bust," Rhonda informs Maggie.

"That's only if I wear heels!"

"Hattie, don't be so sensitive." Clarissa turns to Maggie. "Our quarterback, George Lawson, finally worked up the nerve to ask me this morning. In fact, we've all got football players."

She looks with satisfaction at her entourage.

"But I think there might still be one left for you," Clarissa assures Maggie. "Granted, he's one of the dregs, 'cuz the early bird's already come and gone, but I think he'll do."

Maggie finds this amusing. "There's nothin' I love more than the dregs," she replies.

"I like your positive attitude." Clarissa smiles through clamped teeth and loops her arm through Maggie's.

She and the other girls steer Maggie toward the bandstand where a rowdy group of muscle-bound boys play a brutal game of Bloody Knuckles.

~ ~ ~ ~ ~

Iris, meanwhile, lies face-up on her bed, still wearing her skirt and spectator heels. She's even been careful not to muss her hair, arranging it on her pillow. But the black rivulets of mascara have hardened from her eyes to her chin.

Iris isn't asleep exactly, but she's also not awake. She's in a state that's as familiar as the back of her hand. Numb.

With no warning, the bedroom door flies open and Francie, stone cold sober, marches in.

"What're these?" she demands, holding up the bottle of pills Dr. Kay prescribed Iris earlier in the day. "I found them in your school bag."

Iris stares, unable to speak.

"Iris, I am asking you a question. What in hellfire are these??" She shakes the bottle hard.

"They're ... they're for my bladder, Mama. Maggie took me to the doctor ..."

Francie sneers. "Maggie, Maggie, Maggie. I don't like this girl fillin' your head with all kinds of ideas."

"She's my friend."

"Some friend," she snorts. "You know what these are?"

"Pills for my ..."

"They're sugar!" Francie informs Iris. "That's all these

are. Sugar pills!"

Francie twists the cap off the bottle and shakes a few pills into the palm of her hand.

But Iris doesn't wilt. In fact, she does the opposite, leaping out of bed like a firefighter at the clang of the bell.

"Give me my pills!" Iris demands.

Francie pops some in her mouth, and sucks on them. "Sugar," she says.

"Mama, give me my pills, now!"

Francie doesn't hear the steel in her daughter's voice, nor see the fire in her eyes. She eats a few more of Iris's pills, crunching them with grim satisfaction.

"Give 'em!" Iris grabs the bottle out of Francie's hands, sending a dozen pills skittering across the wooden floor. Iris gets on her hands and knees, chasing them.

"Well, don't go crazy over a buncha sugar pills Iris," Francie says. Then, pointedly. "You'll just wet yourself."

The world stops cold. Iris sits back on her heels, in the still-point. This is when the water should come forth like a flood, drowning her in disgrace.

Iris waits, teeth gritted. And waits. And waits. Finally she turns bold eyes on her mother's.

"I didn't wet myself, Mama. I'm dry. Dry as a bone."

Francie flinches. It's subtle, but it's there: the sting of defeat. She puffs out her chest, ready to do her worst. Only Iris is standing now, too, her shoulders squared.

Unconsciously, Francie steps back. She's never met this Iris before. A girl who has the power of someone who's been seen. Accepted. Loved.

For once, Francie is at a loss of what to do next. Iris,

much to my glee, is not.

She caps her medicine bottle, puts it on her night table, walks to her vanity, as cool as you please, and sits. Reaching for the pressed-powder compact Maggie bought her that very afternoon, Iris begins repairing her makeup.

"What d'you think you're doin'?" Francie asks, a note of uncertainty in her voice.

"I'm goin' to the After-Game dance, Mama."

"That Maggie gal is settin' you up for a fall," Francie sputters. "That she is. And don't you come cryin' to me when it happens!"

Francie storms out of the room, slamming the door behind her. But both Iris and Francie know the balance of power is shifting like quicksand. And one of them is going under.

Chapter Seven

It's late and Jeff's beat. After a day of plowing up corn stalks and oiling Hank's tractor, Jeff's just now coming out of the garage, wiping grease off his hands with a filthy rag. That's when he sees the Deerborne's back door swing wide.

His breath catches in his throat when Iris steps out, a vision of soft lines and gentle colors, heels stepping smartly down the drive.

He feels an unexpected surge of pride to see Iris turned out like this, but he's also worried for her safety since he knows she's near-blind and she isn't wearing her glasses!

Jeff realizes Iris is heading in his direction. Looking at his blackened hands, he ducks back into the shadows. Only when she's passed does Jeff poke his head out, watching Iris walk toward Old Junction Road, head held high.

How I'd love to lead the two of them together by the hand, knowing that each is so ready for the other. But there are limits even the most well-meaning ghost must accept.

~ ~ ~ ~ ~

Clarissa, Rhonda and Hattie present Maggie like a trophy to the liquor-sloppy, noisome boys at the band stand. Clarissa sidles up to the one with jet-black hair and eyes as violet as Elizabeth Taylor's.

She loops her arm through his. "George Lawson," she murmurs, eyes batting. "I hope you don't think you're gonna drink like this on prom night?!"

George throws a sodden arm around Clarissa's neck. "Only if you do, honey."

125

Clarissa beams to her audience. "My mama says a lady never drinks to excess. But I guess I've never been much of a lady."

This gets the desired guffaws from the gang.

"Come here." Clarissa nudges Maggie in front of the only seventeen-year-old boy at WaKeeney High who looks like a full-grown man. A six-four linebacker who can grow a full beard in a week flat, to all the boys' chagrin.

"Craig Butler," Clarissa announces dramatically. "Meet Maggie Richmond."

Craig squints at Maggie down the long shotgun-barrel of inebriation. When he reaches the end, he grins.

"I don't know where you been hidin' her, Clarzibell, but she's pretty as you said she was."

Maggie plays along. "*She's* right here, standing in front of you."

"And feisty too. I like that in my women," Craig laughs, laying a beefy hand on Maggie's shoulder.

She shrugs the hand off. "Not sure I like *obnoxious* in my men," Maggie replies.

Like a curtain falling, the smile drops out of Craig's eyes. Everybody goes silent. The boys' nerves ramp up. Most have been on the receiving end of Craig's hitting, both on and off the field. An angry Craig Butler is a situation best avoided.

Rhonda and Hattie shudder for Maggie, too. Craig may be a cowboy charmer, but they know he doesn't date girls, he beds them. And right now he's looking Maggie up and down as if she was a choice cut of meat.

Bold as she is, Maggie's jaw tightens and a flicker of fear comes to her eyes. It's the same look she gets when Gerald takes off his belt.

Craig sidles up close. Maggie can see manly chest hair curling over the throat of his shirt. She can smell him; musky cedar, sweat and bourbon.

Craig leans down so he can look Maggie in the eye.

"*When* I take you to prom," he murmurs, "I'll be sure to leave 'obnoxious' at home."

Again, Craig slides an arm around Maggie's shoulders, this time giving her a tight squeeze. Maggie steels herself then she leans into Craig's arms, going soft and flirty.

"If you don't, I'm gonna make you wish you did.'

Craig's intensity breaks into a chuckle. "Dayum, this gal's a wildcat. Just how I like 'em."

The group breathes a collective sigh of relief.

"If you two go together, " Clarissa says, "we can take a group picture for the yearbook."

"Maybe Maggie's dad could take it?" Rhonda pipes up. "Since that's his job and all."

"He's pretty busy," Maggie replies.

"Well, you gotta tell him to get unbusy!" Clarissa declares. "Tell him your bosom friends are just as important as any of his celebrities!"

"I'll see what I can do," Maggie grunts, ending it.

"What I wanna know is, where are we gonna eat?" Hattie asks.

"Must food always be your first priority?" Clarissa scolds.

"Well, we have to eat before the dance, don't we?" Hattie pouts. "So that oughta come first!"

Throughout the chatter, Maggie has gone blank. True, she manages to nod her head and "mmm hmmm" at all the right moments — she even hides her mortification when George

Lawson gives poor Derek Wilton a wedgie — but Maggie feels like a cat in a parlor full of rocking chairs.

Her eyes drift without purpose across the banners and balloons, the clusters of dancers, the scrubbed, smiling faces of teens she'll never feel a part of. Then she spies a familiar figure across the dance floor.

Suddenly, Maggie comes to life. Turning to the others she shouts, "I'll be right back! I see a friend!" then flies away.

"Where does she think she's goin'?" Clarissa complains to no one in particular. "We're plannin' our prom itinerary!"

Clarissa's eyes follow Maggie, a line of worry on her brow. What if this "friend" is a WaKeeney Baton Twirler? A group that sometimes steals the Songbirds' choreography! She'll be *damned* if they steal Maggie, too!

Clarissa watches as Maggie approaches a tall, curvy stranger standing at the entrance to the gym. The girl wears a sweet angora sweater and heels Clarissa would love to get her hands on.

With grim satisfaction, she sees the stranger slouching and scowling. Thank goodness. No boy bait there!

Clarissa's just losing interest when Maggie reaches the girl who suddenly straightens and beams. Puzzled, Clarissa watches the two girls embrace. And then her expression narrows.

"Who's that with Maggie?" Craig Butler asks.

"I dunno," Rhonda says, squinting.

"Maybe she's new?" offers Walter Goggins, a rotund center lineman who can't run worth a damn but can block a locomotive.

"It's Iris Deerborne," Clarissa states flatly.

"It is not!" scoffs Brian Embrick, the Panther's defensive end, whose eyeballs are indeed level with Hattie's undeniable bust.

"Yes, it is." Clarissa feigns disinterest. "Can't you smell her?"

"Iris Deerborne?" George Lawson gawks. "Damn, she cleans up good."

"You're delusional," Clarissa snaps.

"If he's delusional then I'm deranged," Brian Embrick hoots. "Who knew Stinky Drawers was actually a girl?"

"Brian, put your eyes back in your head or I'll knock 'em out for good," threatens Hattie.

Rhonda sidles up to Clarissa and whispers in her ear, "Maybe we got Iris wrong?"

"Don't be simple," Clarissa spits then turns to George Lawson. Taking him by the hand, she leans in and plants a lingering kiss along his jawline. "You gonna come dance with me or stare at a girl who wears diapers?"

Clarissa's got his full attention now. "Baby, all I wanna do is dance with you."

~ ~ ~ ~ ~

"I'm so glad you came," Maggie sings as she pulls Iris into the festooned gym.

"Uh huh," Iris manages.

"Is that all you can say?"

"I can barely say that. My throat's dry as dirt."

"Let's get you some punch."

Iris stands rooted to her patch of floor. "I can't move."

"Then I'll go get it."

"No! Just …" her eyes plead, "… just stay with me."

"Let's sit. Can you do that?"

Iris nods and lets Maggie lead her, like a wobbly newborn foal, to the bleachers where the wallflowers wait to dance and the boys refuse to ask.

Maggie holds Iris's arm, as if to keep her from floating away. "What's that scent?" she asks.

"Do I smell bad?" Iris asks, suddenly worried. "I haven't … I didn't …"

Maggie instantly realizes her mistake. "No, no! I meant, what's that perfume you're wearing? It's to die for."

Iris blushes. "'White Shoulders'," she confides, "I stole some from my mama's room on my way out the door."

Maggie laughs. "Serves her right!"

~ ~ ~ ~ ~

On the dance floor, Clarissa counterfeits a smile at her date. But inside, she's fit to be tied bearing witness to that ridiculous, stinking sow, Iris Deerborne, hunched on the bleachers talking to their newest Songbird.

Clarissa's had it! Maggie Richmond might be a somewhat attractive, mildly polished Brand New Thing, but Clarissa's done with her!

It's as obvious as the nose on Clarissa's face that Maggie doesn't care a whit about what it means to be a member of the Songbird family. Which includes keeping the group sacred by not exposing it to bottom-dwellers like Iris.

She should've followed her instincts when she saw Maggie for the first time. She should've avoided the girl who, it's now clear, is nothing more than an over-rated poser of the very lowest caliber.

And what the hell has gotten into Rhonda?

Clarissa watches in disbelief as Rhonda cranes her neck over her dance partner's shoulder to get a better look at Maggie and Iris hob-knobbing.

"What's the matter, Rhonda?" Clarissa seethes. "Those girls owe you money?"

"Huh?"

"Well, you're lookin' at 'em like you want to kiss their lily-white asses!"

"No, I ..."

"Just save it!" Clarissa snarls. Then she sees the second most shocking sight of the night: Jeff Owings (my dear heart) entering the dance!

The cowlicked boy who farms daily, who doesn't care what he wears or who notices, is almost unrecognizable.

His shoulders spread broadly in a pressed, collared shirt tucked into neat dungarees. His hair, brushed into a tidy duck's tail, reveals a noble brow over dark, searching eyes. Shined boots proudly gleam in a sea of sneakers.

Clarissa can't once remember Jeff wearing anything so nice. But here he is, all dolled up. Looking even dreamier than usual.

As he walks over to the bleachers and takes a seat just above Maggie and Iris, Clarissa looks like she's swallowed her shoe.

If he asks that damned Maggie to prom, Clarissa's going to have a grade-A shit fit!

~ ~ ~ ~ ~

"If I go to prom with Mister Cro-Magnon Craig over there," Maggie tells Iris, nodding toward Craig Butler, "it'll

131

get my parents and the Songbirds off my back for a month or so."

Iris nods absently. She pulls at her sweater sleeves and examines the toes of her feet in Grace's shoes. Jeff's sudden closeness has struck her deaf and mute.

Iris has participated in more heart-stopping activities during this one day than in her entire life! But having Jeff practically sitting in her lap takes the cake.

Her heart clangs so loud in her chest she's sure everyone can hear it. Even over Annette Funicello singing "O Dio Mio!".

"Iris!"

Iris startles then looks at her friend, "What?"

"I just told you I got asked to prom by the blockhead in the letterman's jacket. Are you even listening to me?"

Iris attempts an interested look. "Um, yes?"

"Then what'd I say?"

"Um." Iris colors and makes another sleeve adjustment.

"Where'd you go?"

"I … I …"

Jeff speaks. "Hey, Iris."

Two more terrifying and beautiful words Iris has never heard said aloud. Nor been unable to reply to. Maggie nudges her. "That dish behind us is talkin' to you."

"I know," Iris responds with what seems Herculean effort.

Realization dawns. "So that's where your brain's at!" Maggie grins. Then, speaking loud enough for the cheap seats to hear, "Did you say you're thirsty, Iris? No problem. I'll be right back with some punch."

"Maggie … no!"

"I won't be a minute. Or ten."

"Maggie!" Before Iris's myopic, disbelieving eyes, she watches Maggie stand up and — for the love of Pete — walk away!

No, no no no no!!

An interminable silence follows Maggie's departure. Iris feels compelled to fill it with something, with *anything*, but she literally cannot open her paralyzed mouth.

"Did you have to pay?" Jeff asks.

Iris twists her head toward his voice behind her. "Um, what?" she manages.

"Did your mom make you pay for the eggs you dropped?"

"Oh. No." She ventures an eyeball toward his face.

"Well, that's good," Jeff says, "'cuz otherwise I was gonna pay you back."

"Oh." It's all Iris can say. *Where is Maggie, where is Maggie?*

~ ~ ~ ~ ~

On the dance floor, Clarissa leans toward Rhonda and her partner. "Look at Iris droolin' all over Jeff Owings. As if *he'd* ask her to dance!"

"He won't even ask *you* to dance," Rhonda marvels.

"And I wouldn't want him to, with the crazy that runs in his family!"

"I hear it skips a generation," Hattie interjects, swinging past with her partner. "Your kids'd probably hang themselves."

"Too bad about that, 'cuz Jeff's a dreamboat," Rhonda sighs.

Even Clarissa can't argue with that.

~ ~ ~ ~ ~

Just as Iris decides it's safe to turn her head away, Jeff addresses her again. "So … you wanna dance?"

"What?"

Jeff speaks louder. "I was wondering … if you wanna dance?"

"Why?"

"Um, because … it's a dance?" Jeff offers.

"That's okay."

"You don't want to?"

"People will …" Iris starts. "I mean, they'll … Jeff, they'll just laugh at me."

Iris meets Jeff's eye and he hers. "Let 'em try." Jeff holds out his hand. After a moment, Iris takes it.

~ ~ ~ ~ ~

"Sweet Mary Mother of God!" Hattie nearly runs over a couple of two-stepping freshmen as she drags her partner across the dance floor to Clarissa and Rhonda. "Jeff is dancing with Iris!"

"Shut your mouth!" Clarissa, whose back was turned, witnesses the front-headlines of Iris Deerborne swaying clumsily in Jeff Owing's arms — a foot of air between them.

The Songbirds' mouths form silent O's. Meanwhile, Maggie sets down two cups of punch and hooks her arm through Craig Butler's.

"Wanna take me for a spin around the floor?" she asks sweetly, one eye on Iris.

"I'd like to do more than that," Craig grunts.

"Let's start there," Maggie replies drolly.

Watching the Songbirds ogle Iris and Jeff gives Maggie the most delicious satisfaction.

~ ~ ~ ~ ~

"Your eyes look pretty," Jeff tells Iris as they sway, sweaty-handed, back and forth. "I mean, they're pretty with glasses on too. You just can't see 'em the same way."

"I'll have to wear them again. The glasses. It's just for one night," she informs Jeff, though she has no idea how he can see her eyes when they're glued to the third button down on his shirt.

"I didn't ask you to dance 'cuz you weren't wearing your glasses," Jeff says.

Suddenly, Iris stiffens with panic. She looks up quickly to see if anyone is laughing at them. Or worse, nudging Jeff knowingly. Did someone put him up to this?

She can hear Francie's voice in her head, clear as a bell, "Boys like Jeff Owings don't happen to girls like you, Iris, and the sooner you realize that the better off you'll be."

"I'm sorry," Iris says, as she tries to step away from Jeff. "I don't feel so good. I think I need to sit down."

"Oh, sure, sure, I'm sorry." Jeff tries to escort Iris off the dance floor, but she pulls away.

"It's okay. You don't have to come with me. You can go. There are other girls … other girls …"

"I don't care about other girls," Jeff says.

Iris's stare could burn a hole through Jeff's chest. Suddenly, anger blossoms like a flame held to paper.

"Why are you here?" she accuses. "Why are you asking me to dance?"

"'Cuz you're the only girl in this town who isn't a phony," Jeff blurts. "And when I saw you leave the farm tonight … to come here …" his eyes drop, embarrassed. "… it made me realize … just how brave you are. I hope to be that brave someday … about the things that are hard for me."

Iris looks up, right into Jeff's eyes. The orphan stands before her, not the enigmatic loner.

Without thinking, she puts a hand to his face, the way she did when they were cradle-mates, and bears witness to his unshed tears.

In the gym, under the blanket of twinkling lights, before the gaze of a hundred people who don't matter anymore, Iris moves back into Jeff's arms.

As they dance before the world and God, Iris knows she loves him. Simple as that. She loves him and it's a true thing. Iris lets herself feel it, because in that moment she knows it won't destroy her. It won't cost her a thing if he never loves her back.

~ ~ ~ ~ ~

The Songbirds have abandoned their dance partners. They stand stock still in the middle of the dance floor openly gaping at Jeff and Iris with jealousy. And grudging admiration.

"Maybe …" Hattie whispers to the girls, "Maybe … Iris Deerborne is deep after all?"

Chapter Eight

Monday morning, as Iris digs into her school locker, a female voice hollers, "Hey, Iris."

She looks up to see Hattie McCoy sashay past, her bounteous hips on a swivel.

Iris wears her glasses, but she wonders if they're working because she thinks she saw Hattie smile and wink at her.

~ ~ ~ ~ ~

In chemistry, Miss Steingarten switches Clarissa's partner from Iris to Jonna Deese, the girl best known for playing trombone through a mouth full of metal in the WaKeeney Panthers' marching band.

"I don't see why I have to swap partners smack dab in the middle of the semester," Clarissa complains.

"Honestly, Clarissa," cries Miss Steingarten, "You need to pick a position and stick to it. You can't keep changing your mind all the time!"

"Well, just when I get used to Iris, you gotta switch everything," Clarissa pouts.

She shoots Iris an aggrieved look, forcing Iris to remove her glasses and clean them as thoroughly as possible with the edge of her sweater.

~ ~ ~ ~ ~

At noon, Iris eats from her sack lunch under a scraggly red maple on the outskirts of the student quad.

She's reading Daphne Du Maurier's gothic romance *Rebecca* — (I'm glad she's partial to ghost stories) — when Rhonda Robertson plops down across from Iris as if she'd done it every day.

137

"You seen Clarissa?" Rhonda asks, pulling a Thermos of tomato soup out of her lunch box.

Iris stares at Rhonda like she's got sow teats on her forehead.

"She said she might ditch third and go to the Dairy Queen," Rhonda continues.

"Oh." Confused, Iris returns to her book.

Suddenly, Rhonda hollers, "Hattie, we're over here!"

Iris feels like she's in a *Twilight Zone* episode where she's swapped lives with an identical twin in a parallel universe.

Hattie arrives and flops down right next to Iris. "Omigod, it's hot as Hades at this table. Why'd you have to sit right smack in the burning sun, Rhonda?"

"So we can get a tan before prom," Rhonda says. "Right, Iris?"

Iris manages a shrug.

Rhonda looks at Iris, wanting more. "Did anybody ask you yet?"

"We saw you dancin' with Jeff Owings last night," Hattie presses.

Iris looks up, startled. "Oh, no, no, Jeff wouldn't ask me."

"He hasn't asked anybody else!" Hattie assures her.

"Susan Stradall is fit to be tied," Rhonda crosses herself. "She thought this year, for sure, he'd ask her. God knows she's been workin' on him since kindergarten."

"She can think again," Hattie mumbles through a mouth full of egg-salad sandwich. "He never goes to prom anyway. He's the lone-wolf type."

"That may be," Rhonda agrees, but puts a reassuring hand on Iris's shoulder. "Don't worry, I'll have Clarissa put in a good word with Jeff. That oughta do the trick."

Iris unthinkingly takes an enormous bite of her peanut butter sandwich. For long moments a case of no-milk mortar-mouth makes it impossible to respond.

Hattie and Rhonda interpret Iris's silence as part of her new profound persona.

~ ~ ~ ~ ~

Later that afternoon, as Iris crosses the student parking lot on her way to the open road, Maggie's car pulls up beside her, crammed with Songbirds.

Clarissa leans out the passenger window. "Hey Iris, you wanna ride?"

Iris shoots a questioning look to Maggie in the driver's seat. The new girl can't hide her cat-who-ate-the-canary grin.

~ ~ ~ ~ ~

"Whoop!" Maggie's head breaks the surface of Sumner Pond. She spits water into the warm, midnight air as Iris strips to her underwear on the shoreline.

"Come on," Maggie bellows from the middle of the pond. "You can't tell me you didn't love having those girls lick your boots!"

"I didn't love it. And sooner or later their gonna find out your daddy doesn't work for *Life* magazine. And then what?"

"If that's all they find out, I'm lucky," Maggie says, treading water. "Besides, my daddy's magazine's owned by *Life*."

"It's still a lie," Iris scolds. "You can't keep lyin' like that!"

139

Maggie thrusts her arm out of the drink in a Scout's Honor salute.

"I swear, Iris Deerborne, I'll never lie to you. But, it was worth it, watching their fat, judgey faces squirm when I told 'em my dad thought you were 'deep.'"

Iris is incredulous. "Me? Deep?"

Maggie cackles with glee.

Iris is about to wade into the water when she sees the ghostly reflection of her sensible, worn-out bra on its surface. She makes a decision and unhooks it.

"Hey! What're you doing?" Maggie shouts, mimicking Iris. "You shouldn't be naked! What if someone comes and sees you?"

Iris grins, mimicking Maggie. "I thought you said this place was private. Who's gonna see me but you?"

Iris sheds her bra and underwear. She stands pale and radiant beneath the beaming moon. She's just about to jump in the pond when Maggie stops her.

"Wait," Maggie says.

"What?"

Maggie looks at her thoughtfully, giving Iris the full measure of her truth. "You're beautiful," she says.

And Iris, perched on the edge of acceptance, feels beautiful.

~ ~ ~ ~ ~

Usually the Richmond family is on full alert when Gerald comes to the breakfast table dressed for work. But today he enters relaxed and smiling.

"I understand a certain young lady has a date to prom?" he says to Maggie.

Grace turns a tight grin toward her daughter. "Candy Butler phoned this morning to tell me her son, Craig, asked you and I just mentioned it to your father because I knew how pleased he'd be."

Gerald beams. "I'm happy you're learning to adjust … making new inroads. I know it isn't easy for you."

"It's okay," Maggie shrugs.

"Does she have to kiss the boy who takes her to prom?" Tallulah pipes up, scandalized.

"She's gotta let him get to second base!" Emmett informs his sibling.

"That's disgusting!" shrieks Tallulah. "Mom, Emmett's being disgusting!"

"Grace," Gerald barks at his wife. "Have you been watching the afternoon soaps again? Because that's where the twins get this stuff!"

"Not since you put your foot down, sweetheart." Grace tries to change the subject. "Candy says Craig's a football player. Isn't that nice, he plays football?"

"Well, sure," Gerald turns to Maggie. "I thought you could skip school today and look for a dress with your mother?"

"Could I come too?" Tallulah begs.

"No, honey, this is Maggie's day," Grace replies.

"Why is it never my day? And when it is, I have to share it with Emmett?"

"Don't worry, Lula." Maggie smiles at her. "I can't go anyway. I have a quiz in Classics."

"I think it'd be a nice thing to do. Look for a dress," Gerald presses. "It's a nice thing mothers and daughters do together."

Looking at her father's face, open and approving for once, Maggie gives in. She puts her napkin down. "I guess I can make up the exam on Monday."

"Good. Good!" Grace chirps. "I'll just go get ready!" She flutters from the room.

Tallulah and Emmett have fallen to playing paper-rock-scissors, unaware of the weighted silence between Maggie and Gerald.

After a moment, he offers his brand of kindness. "And don't worry about money, Margot. You just get what you want. No expense spared."

"Thanks, Dad."

~ ~ ~ ~ ~

Hazel Atkins is dog tired. It's five o' clock on Friday and she's spent the last four hours fixing a peroxide-gone-wrong.

Madge Tittle, WaKeeney's irascible librarian, decided to save a dollar-fifty by getting her bleach done at the Snip-It chain down on Barclay Avenue.

An hour later, without an appointment, Madge took what was now her orange dome to Hazel who had to hurry her set-and-dry clients out the door to save Madge's hair.

In the end, Hazel'd had to lop off a good five inches and was rewarded with nothing but ire.

"Hazel," Madge had said, fuming at what was left of her hair. "I certainly hope you don't think I'm gonna *pay* you for pluckin' me like a chicken!"

"I wouldn't think of it, Miss Tittle," Hazel said, knowing full well the librarian's hot temper and wide influence.

She's now sweeping up the last clippings of Madge's burnt locks when Maggie's Packard races up.

Hazel watches the coltish girl hop out of her car and head toward the salon, carrying a large white box under her arm. Hazel looks away and busies herself with the dustpan.

The bell rings brightly as Maggie bursts into the salon bringing movement and life to the dreary day.

"Please tell me you're not closed already?" Maggie begs. She indicates the white box, "This *THING* has been foisted on me and I've got to find a way to make it work."

"Well, I was gonna call it an early day," Hazel replies over her shoulder. "But this sounds like an emergency."

She sets her broom and dustpan aside. "What can I do for you, sweetie? And start from the beginning."

"I just got a date to the prom," Maggie says, fidgeting with the box. "Guess who picked the dress?"

"Let's see it."

Maggie lifts the lid of the white box to reveal a candy-apple-red gown seeded in textured lace with a plunging halter-neck meant for hourglass figures.

Hazel takes in Maggie's checked capris pants, collared white shirt and black Capezio flats. The girl looks ready to jump on a Vespa and take a spin around the Trevi Fountain.

Hazel laughs. "I think your mom picked the dress."

"Does Grace — my mother — mistake me for Sophia Loren? Because *that's* Grace. She's Sophia Loren all the way. I'm basically a tall boy. What is it with mothers and prom dresses? 'Cuz from where I'm sittin' it's an epidemic. And there's more ..."

"How is that possible?"

143

"Grace says I need a stylish haircut to go with the dress. I'm not sure what kinda haircut qualifies as 'stylish,' but I think she means short."

Hazel smiles. "I can't imagine why she'd want you to do that. Just about every woman I know would kill to have hair that looks like spun gold and stays thick when it's so long."

Maggie sighs. "Could you tell my mom that?"

"I'd be happy to."

"Good. Then maybe you could just set it and give me an updo the day of?"

Hazel hesitates. "Might be a squeeze," she says. "Half the town wants to come in that day. But maybe we could try something now and I could show you how to do it yourself?"

"That'd be great!"

"Since you didn't get to choose the dress, you'll definitely want to choose the hair. Come sit," Hazel pats a chair.

Maggie closes the lid over the dress and parks herself before the large mirror.

Hazel releases Maggie's hair from its rubber band and brushes it, observing the state of it with a professional eye. "I do think we should trim a few split ends before we decide on a style."

"Okay."

Hazel starts snipping. "So, how're you liking WaKeeney?"

"It's got its positives and its negatives."

"The positives being Iris?"

Maggie nods. "And the negatives being everybody else!"

"I felt that way when I moved here a year ago," Hazel sighs. "It's hard bein' new in a place where everybody's known each other's business since the dawn of man."

"So, you like it here now?"

"Well, I wouldn't go that far," Hazel laughs, holding out a lock to snip. "But I inherited the house and salon last year and I needed a fresh start, so here I am."

Maggie wonders at her. "You needed a fresh start?"

"That I did."

"Not gonna tell me?"

"Nope."

Maggie chuckles. Then goes silent. After a long minute, she says quietly. "I needed a fresh start too."

"How's that part going?" Hazel asks kindly.

"The jury's out," Maggie sighs.

"We have a lot in common." Hazel smiles at Maggie in the mirror.

"If you could live anywhere," Maggie asks, "where would it be?"

Hazel looks up, considering.

"Anywhere outside Kansas would be a thrill," she says, clipping. "Coming from Blue Mound — which has about five people and three dogs — I'd love a true city. But one right next to the ocean, like Manhattan or Los Angeles. I've never seen the ocean."

Maggie warms to that. "Oh, you've got to! My folks took me to the Jersey Shore when I was six and I got to stick my feet in the Atlantic. It was like gettin' an electric shock, the water was so cold. And the tide'd like to rip me right out to sea. Scared the bejesus out of me," she laughs. "But at the same time, it made me feel like I was … I don't know … wide awake."

Hazel grins at Maggie's exuberance. "You've got me convinced. There's somethin' about being landlocked that feels … I don't know … parched and fenced-in."

"'Parched' and 'fenced-in.' You're a poet."

Hazel gives Maggie a wry look. "I'm bookish. Which isn't a great thing to be in Blue Mound. Or WaKeeney, for that matter."

Hazel twists Maggie's hair into a knot at the nape.

"What d'you think about this? We could go for a chignon to give you that Audrey Hepburn look."

"That kinda gives me a headache."

"It's 'cuz you have so much hair, lucky girl."

She takes down the knot and splits Maggie's hair on either side of her face.

"Dorothy in *The Wizard of Oz*?"

Maggie pushes her hair up into a bob.

"Annette Funicello in *Zorro*. All I need's a bullet bra and somethin' to fill it with."

Hazel doesn't smile. She gently combs Maggie's hair down natural, smoothing it with her hand.

"I like it this way," she says. "Unadorned. Like you."

Their eyes meet in the mirror. Hazel abruptly releases Maggie's hair and stashes the brush away.

"You don't really need a hairstyle," Hazel says, quickly shutting the drawer. "Maybe I can get Mrs. Bailey to come in and do you for a set and dry the day of? A lot of times she helps if I'm overbooked."

Maggie looks down and gets out of the chair. "That sounds good."

Hazel walks to her appointment book and opens it, scanning the page as Maggie waits, shifting from foot to foot.

"Let me see. The dance starts at seven?"

"Yes."

"Mrs. Bailey's chaperoning, so I probably can't get her to stay past five. Can you come in at three-thirty?"

"Sure."

Hazel smiles faintly. "You'll have to leave with a bag over your carefully styled head and be sure to not move 'til seven o' clock."

Maggie nods. She grabs her dress box. "Thanks for helping, Hazel. I really appreciate it."

As she heads for the door, Maggie spots the photograph of Hazel's former love in his soldier's uniform. She picks it up. "Do you ever miss him?" Maggie asks quietly.

Hazel looks up from her book. She hesitates when she sees what Maggie's holding. "I do. He was a kind soul."

"Think you'll ever fall in love again?"

Hazel opens her mouth, about to say what's expected. "Of course," "I hope so," "If I'm lucky." But it's been a long year of speaking half-truths. And they feel all wrong in this company.

"I was never in love with him *that* way," Hazel murmurs, shutting her notebook. "When I moved here, that's just what I told people. In a small town, people want to know everything, so they can put you in a little box. So you make sense to them. So they can feel ... I don't know ... like they can define you."

147

She walks closer to Maggie, who hasn't moved. "Folks 'round here are a lot more comfortable with a broken-hearted girl who lost her love in the war than a single woman who never wants to marry," Hazel murmurs.

Maggie looks down at the framed photograph. "Who is he?"

Hazel gazes at the boy with bittersweet affection.

"My little brother, Scott. He was nineteen when he left for Korea. Just a kid. So skinny his uniform hung off him like a gunny sack on a broomstick. And he had these horrible spots all over his forehead."

She gives a rueful smile. "Poor Scott thought he'd never get a girl with that bad skin. And boy, was he desperate for a girl!" Hazel wipes away fast tears. "The worst part, for me, is that he didn't get a chance to outgrow that ... that notion of himself as a flawed person."

Hazel doesn't dare look at Maggie, but when she reaches to take the photo from her, their hands touch.

The space between them comes alive. Hazel can't stop herself. As she looks into Maggie's quiet, understanding eyes, her hand moves independent of her will and cups Maggie's cheek.

Maggie leans into Hazel's hand as if she's come home.

Hazel's breath goes shallow. Pinpricks of fear dot her neck and chest. She pulls her hand away, as from a hot stove, and steps back.

In a moment, she's turned away and retrieved her broom and dustpan.

"See you at three-thirty prom night, sweetie," Hazel says in a neutral tone, as she sets to sweeping imaginary hair from the parlor floor.

"Great." Maggie replies, her throat thickening. "So. Goodbye."

"Goodbye," Hazel responds, without looking back.

Hazel hears the bell tinkle as Maggie leaves. She closes her eyes tight, puts a hand to her brow, then, moment by moment, composes herself as she listens to the sound of Maggie's car driving fast, then faster away.

~ ~ ~ ~ ~

Late that night Maggie breaks into Gerald's liquor cabinet. Gerald and Grace don't drink, but like all good hosts, Maggie's folks keep a cache of the top-shelf brands on hand — and like all good parents, keep them under lock and key.

Neither fact has ever affected Maggie in the slightest since liquor has never been her rebellion of choice.

Until tonight.

Tonight she has the haunted look of a hunted animal. Her hands shake as she shoves a bobby pin into the liquor cabinet lock.

In five minutes she's fled the house with a flask of Four Roses in her grip, leaving a bobby pin still jammed in the keyhole.

~ ~ ~ ~ ~

It's nigh on midnight in deserted downtown WaKeeney, and Craig Butler's looking for a fight.

He's with George Lawson, Brian Embrick and Walter Goggins at a local diner called The Onion, which rolled its shutters down an hour ago.

Apparently, Craig's got just enough 100 proof liquor in his gullet to make him want to swing at someone, and it doesn't much matter who.

Normally, this ugly mood finds its outlet at a small colored community halfway to Hays, where Craig and his boys can usually find some poor soul to jump.

But Craig's '49 Studebaker fossil only made it as far as the diner before conking out. And Craig's already got a bloody fist from punching dents in the dashboard.

Now he's looking for something else to hit, and it may have to be one of his boys.

Craig's bleary eyes land on Walter first, then move on. That sumbitch can hold his own and might even take Craig out.

He glances past Brian, who's just too damned short to make it interesting.

Then Craig starts sizing up Pretty-Boy Lawson. The girls call Lawson's blue eyes "violet." *Like pansies*, Craig thinks. He wonders what those eyes'd look with a couple a' swollen lids?

But Lawson's in luck. His eyes will live to see another lavender day, because Maggie Richmond's Packard veers past at exactly that moment.

A squeal of brakes bites the air as Maggie skids to a stop, throws the gear stick in reverse, then backs up unsteadily to the group.

"Craig Butler ... is that you?" she shouts through the passenger window.

Craig struggles to focus, then grins. "Well, lookie here, and just when I thought it was gonna be a wasted night."

"Listen, Mister Man," Maggie scolds. "I don't recall saying yes to prom night with you! Yet my mama made me buy a dress today 'cuz your mama says you're takin' me!"

Craig sidles over and thrusts his broad, grown-man face in her open passenger window, testing his cowboy charm.

"You sure are a sight for sore eyes, but am I mistaken or are you shit-canned?"

Craig nods to the flask on the seat of the Packard. Maggie ignores the question, answering charm for charm.

"I don't think it's nice tellin' everyone you're takin' a gal to a dance when she never did say yes," she pouts. "Don't I have the right to make up my own mind?"

"I figure I know what's good for you," Craig drawls, winking.

"Think so?"

"Know so."

"Prove it."

Craig sends a knowing grin back to his boys, who hoot on cue. George Lawson gives him the thumbs up as Craig climbs into the passenger seat next to Maggie. She shoots him a crooked smile.

"Here's somethin' to put a little hair on your chest," she mumbles, offering Craig the flask.

"I got enough hair on my chest," he replies, casually throwing an arm around her.

"I noticed." She tips the flask.

"Where'd you get this hooch?"

"All I know," Maggie says, "is there might be a bottle of Four Roses in my dad's liquor cabinet that's filled to the brim with water."

This earns a lopsided grin from Craig. "I like the way you operate."

He takes the flask as Maggie steps on the gas, leaving downtown WaKeeney in a plume of exhaust.

~ ~ ~ ~ ~

Sumner Pond is a symphony of bullfrogs and crickets, harmonizing in croaks and chirps. But nature's tranquility is soon disrupted by the cackling, hollering mayhem of Maggie and Craig crashing through underbrush into the clearing.

They share what's left of her flask as they stumble to shore.

It takes a moment for Craig to realize where they are.

"Jesus, Maggie," he slurs, wiping his mouth, "why'd you have to bring me to this shithole?"

Maggie gazes off. "I think it's kinda beautiful. Peaceful."

"If you like rottin' bodies floatin' around under your feet," Craig hollers, squinting anxiously into the shadows. He looks down at Maggie. "What's wrong with you, girl? You gotta dark side?"

"As a matter of fact, I do," Maggie concedes, draining the remainder of the flask.

That gets Craig's attention. "Hey, hey, hey! You're not gonna share the last drop with me?"

"Nope." Maggie wipes her mouth with the back of her hand and chucks the flask into the pond where it glug-glug-glugs to the mucky bottom.

As Maggie watches the flask's ripples fade, Craig plants himself behind her, pressing the full length of his body against hers. His hands beginning to explore.

Maggie braces herself, eyes closed, holding perfectly still. But when Craig turns her to face him and shoves one hand down the back of her capris, Maggie's eyes fly open in a sudden, sober panic.

"I don't think this is such a good idea!" she says, feigning lightness as she Houdinis out of Craig's arms.

Befuddled by her sudden absence, Craig hollers, "Hey! Where you goin' ... what ... what d'you say?"

"You're right," Maggie shuffles backward. "We shouldn't be here. It's too creepy."

Craig's eyes light up with renewed temper. "You told me to prove I know what's good for you and I aim to do it."

In two quick strides, Craig closes the distance between them and cages Maggie in a steely grip.

Her hands brace against his chest, pushing with all their might. It's like trying to push a mountain.

Craig's mouth crushes Maggie's. His teeth scrape her tongue. And then, just like that, Maggie surrenders, sinking down and down and down, like a very sad woman in a heavy black coat.

She knows she shouldn't. Knows she's a fighter. But Maggie's found what she was looking for. The same thing she sought in her daddy's liquor cabinet. Oblivion. She knots her fists in Craig's hair and kisses him like she's going to war.

Craig pushes her to the ground and rolls her beneath him. Maggie tastes blood in her mouth, then closes her eyes.

She doesn't open them for a very long time.

~ ~ ~ ~ ~

Loud, insistent tapping rouses Iris from a deep sleep. Confused, she looks about wildly until she realizes someone's tapping on her second-floor bedroom window.

Iris fumbles on her night table for her glasses, crams them on and stumbles from bed. She pulls open the gingham curtains, yelping when she comes nose-to-nose with Maggie through the windowpane.

153

"Lemme in!" Maggie shouts.

Iris quickly pushes up the window sash. "Maggie! What're you doing here? What time is it?"

Iris looks around for her clock as Maggie struggles to get over the window sill. "Lemme in before I fall off your roof and break my goddamned neck, for Chrissakes!"

"Okay, okay!" Iris reaches for her.

"I got it. I got it!" Maggie shouts, waving Iris off.

She throws one leg through the window and spills into the bedroom, breaking into a fit of giggles as she hits the floor.

Iris flusters around her like an alarmed hen. "Shhh! Maggie, it's three in the morning! If Mama hears you there'll be hell to pay!"

Maggie snorts. "There's always hell to pay, Iris. Didn't you know that?"

Iris's nose wrinkles. She leans in, catching Maggie's bourbon breath. "You're drunk!" And with Francie for a mother, Iris should know.

"I don't think that's accurate." Maggie tries to look wry.

"You smell like ... what is that?"

"Lighter fluid." Maggie bursts into another bout of laughter.

Iris tries to think. "I'll get you some water," she says, uncertain. "Or maybe what you need is coffee?"

Maggie grabs for Iris, capturing her elbow, "No, don't go. Don't go. I don't need anything to drink. It'll just get me drunker!"

Iris kneels next to her. "Why're you drunk? Where've you been?"

"I been to hell, Iris ..." Maggie giggles. "I saw the devil and he said, 'Maggie Richmond, you don't fool me. You ain't got nobody fooled, leastwise myself. I knows my spawn when I sees it ...'"

Maggie's laughter is a runaway train. She can't catch her breath.

"Maggie, shhh, my mama ..!" Iris pleads.

Like a crushing wave, Maggie's laughter turns to weeping, and weeping to sobs. Horrified, Iris turns Maggie to face her.

"What is it? What's wrong?"

"Hey, Iris ..." Maggie can't look at her. "It's just that ... it don't matter if I have different hair ... or clothes ... it's still me. I'm still the same girl I always was. No matter if my daddy moves me out of the big city, the evil city with all those bad influences ... no matter if I'm sick in the soul and need saving ..." Her voice rises in despair. "No matter if I take Craig Butler to Sumner Pond ..."

"Maggie!"

"No matter if he puts himself up inside me and touches me everywhere with those big old football hands ..." Maggie punches at her thighs, her stomach, her chest. "No matter, I can't get it out! I'm dirty and I can't get it out of me!"

Iris can say nothing. This beautiful Viking who hurls rocks the way gods hurl lightning bolts cannot be the broken girl on Iris's bedroom floor.

A thread of steel crawls up Iris's spine. She grabs Maggie's shoulders and pulls her into a strong embrace, cradling her.

"It's okay, Maggie," she vows. "I'm here. You're safe. Just be still."

Iris rocks Maggie as if she were her very own child. "Shh shh shh ... shh shh shh ..."

Maggie's body softens. "You're the only one who sees ... the only one who sees me," Maggie weeps, quieter now. Almost calm.

Iris strokes the hair off Maggie's face. "Of course, I see you," she says with simple truth. "You shine."

Maggie looks into Iris's loving face. She leans up and presses her lips to Iris's lips.

Both girls stop there. One needing salvation, the other frozen in shock.

Maggie leans closer without thinking. Iris pulls her face away. "Maggie ... I ..."

Maggie sees her friend's confusion. Instantly, her face contorts into a mask of shame. She pushes away from Iris and staggers to her feet.

"Nothing happened." Maggie backs up, bumps into the wall.

Iris watches, helpless. "Maggie, it's okay ..."

Maggie bolts to the window, throws a leg through.

Iris jumps to her feet. "Maggie, don't go!"

Maggie turns hopeless eyes on Iris. "Nothing happened, Iris. Nothing happened. I'm sorry. I didn't mean to."

"Maggie, don't go. Please."

"It's not like that with you!" Maggie's voice breaks, "I swear, it's never been like that with you. Do you believe me?"

Iris is mute, for fear she'll say the wrong thing.

"Please, tell me you believe me!" Maggie begs.

156

"I believe you. I believe you!"

Relief floods Maggie's face. "Good. That's good."

Then Maggie's out the window. Out of sight. For a moment, Iris is stupefied. Until fear slices through her and she rushes to the window.

"Maggie, where're you goin'? Maggie!"

But her friend's gone, fast as a river storm that dries up in the blink of an eye, leaving nothing behind but a fallow, dark night.

Chapter Nine

The next morning's sun finds Iris sprawled across her bed like a gut-shot soldier. She'd spent the better part of the night tossing and turning, feeling like she'd failed her true friend.

She's mired in regret for all the things she could have said or done, and for not knowing how to have said or done anything differently.

No matter. Iris throws off her covers with renewed determination. She'll figure it out today. Somehow, she'll set things straight with Maggie.

~ ~ ~ ~ ~

Jeff pulls into the Deerborne front yard on his motorbike with an untucked shirt and cowlicks running wild across his brow. He's surprised to see Iris sitting on the front porch stoop, dressed for school. She's usually gone by this time.

It's been a week since they danced in the high-school gym and they haven't crossed paths since.

Truth be told — and I *do* know the truth — Jeff's been dodging Iris. Not because he didn't want to see her. He's been pining for her company. But he knew the next time they met, he'd have to tell Iris something he wasn't ready for her to know.

Yet here she is, which makes now as good a time to tell as any. Best to rip the Band-Aid off quick.

Jeff hops off his bike. "Mornin'!" he says, casually as he can muster.

"Mornin'," Iris replies absently.

"Hope I didn't get you sick," Jeff says. "I had a bad flu all week. Which is why I haven't been here or at school." Jeff's eyes blink when he lies. "You been okay?"

"I been fine."

"That's a relief. I been sicker than a dog and worried maybe I gave you somethin'."

Iris shrugs and looks past him. Jeff, struck by nerves, shoves his hands in his pockets.

"I had a really good time at the dance the other night," he ventures.

"Uh huh."

Now he licks his lips, concerned. "Iris, are you mad at me?"

Just then, like a worm in the apple, Francie blights any possibility of sweetness, stepping onto the porch with a cup of black coffee and her cigarette. A lacy, pearl-pink slip artfully peeks out from between the folds of her open robe.

"Jeff Owings, there you are!" she coos brightly. "I haven't seen you in a month of Sundays, seems like. You're sure a sight for sore eyes."

Jeff jams his hands deeper. "Mornin', Mrs. Deerborne."

Francie waves her coffee cup at him. "Why don't you just call me Francie, for cryin' out loud. 'Mrs. Deerborne' makes me feel about a hundred years old."

She notes Iris perched on the stoop. "Girl, you best get on to school 'fore you're late."

Iris doesn't look up. "I'm waitin' for my ride."

"Well, it don't look like the cat's pajamas Maggie Richmond is comin'," Francie says with barely hidden satisfaction. "Maybe she's moved on to greener pastures … it happens."

That Francie knows just where to jab Iris, whose face seeps color 'til it's the palest of white.

My boy narrows his eyes at Francie. "I'm her ride today, Mrs. Deerborne." He strides to Iris. "Come on, you're comin' with me."

Jeff holds out his hand. Iris looks up and gladly takes it. He pulls her to her feet, his heart swelling to see Iris stand with her head held high before that woman.

They walk to Jeff's motorbike. He swings a leg over the seat and jumps it to life.

But Francie's got one more arrow in her quiver. "Iris is too heavy to ride on that thing," she says. "Those bikes're made for a lighter frame."

Jeff turns to Francie, his hands white-knuckled on the handlebars. "Motorcycles are made for *young* people, Mrs. Deerborne," he says. "Come on, Iris, get on."

Iris climbs aboard like she's been doing it forever.

"Hang on tight," Jeff shouts. Iris puts her arms around his waist and leans her head against his broad back.

Jeff revs the engine once for good measure and they're off like a shot down that long, parched highway, leaving nothing but dust clouds for Francie's pleasure.

She takes a fierce drag off her cigarette before dropping it to the ground and smashing it under her slippered foot.

~ ~ ~ ~ ~

As WaKeeney High comes into view, Jeff slows his bike and pulls off to the side of the road. For a bitter second, Iris registers hurt, hearing that old, familiar voice say he's afraid to be seen with her. But then she remembers the gym; how he danced with her in front of everyone.

When Jeff gets off the bike, Iris follows. "What's goin' on? Why'd you stop?" she asks.

Jeff turns and sees her soft, wondering face.

"I been wantin' to tell you somethin'." My boy's telltale hands burrow in his pockets. "It's somethin' I don't wanna say there." He nods toward school. "And it might make you mad at me. Maybe not wanna be around me ... I don't know, but I don't want there to be a secret between us."

Iris nods. "Okay."

"Last April the twenty-ninth was my mom's birthday. She would've been forty-two. I hadn't been to Sumner Pond since ... well ... since before she died." Jeff can't look at Iris. He can only look at the ground. "But there was no other place I could go to talk to her ... 'cept that place. And I needed to talk to her, 'cuz I miss her more every year, 'stead of less ... and then I saw you there, floating in the water."

Jeff pushes back his cowlicks, trying to give his hands something to do.

"I know I should've looked away because ... well, you were ... you know ... just in your underthings. But I couldn't, 'cuz you looked so ... happy there. It was like you were ... free ... like you were safe."

Jeff can't stop himself. He looks into Iris's eyes. He needs her to know. "And suddenly, with you bein' there, that place didn't seem so black-awful-bad no more ... 'cuz you looked so at peace. And I thought, maybe, I don't know ... maybe she's at peace too?"

Iris watches Jeff's tears finally fall, silent penitents bearing a sin that isn't theirs.

Thank God my girl, without hesitation, crosses the distance between them, takes hold of Jeff's face and kisses him so tenderly a sunken mother is buoyed by gratitude.

After, Jeff whispers, his face pressed against Iris's hair. "I went back a few more times to see you there. But then I stopped. I didn't want to ruin it for you. I didn't want to steal your magic. I want you to always go there."

Iris gently touches his face. The world shrinks down to the two of them. But in WaKeeney, that's just never going to last.

"Iris, there you are!" Iris and Jeff jump apart like electric cables after the spark as Hattie McCoy idles next to them in her dad's Plymouth.

"Hi, Jeff!" Hattie winks.

"Hi, Hattie," Jeff stammers.

Hattie shouts through the window, "Hey, Iris! Hop in the car, I got somethin' exciting to tell ya!"

"I can't right now," she says, eyes on Jeff.

"That's okay," Jeff responds, feeling a rush of shyness. He climbs back on his bike, then turns his raw face to Iris. "I'll see you later? Maybe after school … if that's okay?"

"Yes," she says simply.

Jeff nods, then jumpstarts his bike and zooms off. Hattie watches him go as Iris settles into the car.

"That boy's got more charisma than if James Dean and Natalie Wood had a baby," Hattie sighs. "Now, guess what happened! Guess!"

Iris shrugs. Hattie takes that as an invitation. "Maggie called me this morning to tell me Craig Butler gave her a ring last night!"

162

Not even Francie at her worst could give Iris a better gut-check.

"A ring? They're getting married?" she blurts.

"No, silly. A ring. A promise ring."

"A promise to what?"

Hattie clearly has the wrong audience.

"Honest to God, Iris, if you're so deep, how come you don't know what a promise ring is?" she cries, exasperated.

In the distance, they hear the school bell clang.

"Cripes! Miss Steingarten's gonna cook my goose if I'm late to chemistry again!" Hattie cries, stomping on the gas.

~ ~ ~ ~ ~

A hand — whose fourth finger boasts a pearl and silver ring — pinches a fluttering butterfly by one wing in Mr. Bangert's Bio 101.

Maggie, wearer of said ring, hasn't the gumption to pin the butterfly to her Styrofoam board and neither does Iris, sitting across from her.

Meanwhile, Clarissa and Rhonda pin frantic butterflies to their boards like they're sticking needles in pin cushions during Home Ec.

It's not just the ring that's new on Maggie. Her usually free-wheeling mane is coiled in a tight, chic bun. Her makeup's a flawless, shiny mask.

She's mid-story and smiles in a way Iris doesn't like as she regales the others with each detail of the moment Craig Butler gave her his ring.

"... and he somehow managed to bootleg a bottle of Dom."

"Dom?" Rhonda asks.

163

"Perignon," Maggie clarifies.

"That's champagne, pinhead," Clarissa informs Rhonda.

Maggie holds her hand before her face, gazing at the ring. "It belonged to Craig's Grandma Nettie. It wasn't her diamond, of course, but it's real pearl!"

Iris stares. She's never met *this* Maggie before. "That ring looks new to me," Iris challenges.

Maggie's eyes wax brighter. "I shined it up with some toothpaste, but it's a bona-fide antique."

With grim determination, Maggie pins her butterfly.

~ ~ ~ ~ ~

Hazel Atkins sits in a booth at The Onion wearing a pressed day dress. A flower-embossed basket purse perches on the bench beside her.

Lately, Hazel's been scheduling lunch breaks on workdays, just to escape the endless flow of peroxide and nail polish.

For a while, she'd just sit in the pedicure chair, devouring a tuna salad sandwich after hanging a droll "Gone Eating" sign on the salon door.

But now she's treating herself as if she had a life beyond her beautician's smock. That means a proper dress and a proper lunch in town.

Company would be nice, of course. But most of her clients are church members, wives and mothers in the middle of childrearing. Hazel is none of those things.

Still, Hazel is content with her solo lunches. She's alone, but less lonely.

Hazel is digging into her Cobb salad when Maggie Richmond's Packard pulls up to the diner window. Maggie sits at the wheel with Clarissa Dell next to her and three girls Hazel can't make out in back.

Before Hazel can look away, her eyes meet Maggie's. But the girl who visited Hazel's salon is gone. A hard blankness has dropped over the brightness in those eyes. Hazel looks away and takes a long pull of her iced tea.

~ ~ ~ ~ ~

In the Packard, Maggie sits up a little higher, wrenching her eyes away from Hazel.

Clarissa opens the passenger door, climbs out and shouts, "Rhonda, Hattie, come on. I can't carry all the take-out by myself!"

Rhonda and Hattie climb out, grousing and grumbling, slamming the passenger door shut, leaving Iris and Maggie alone inside.

All morning, Maggie has ducked Iris, issuing a sing-song "Gotta go!" in the hallways and "Can't talk, I'm late!" at her locker.

Now Iris leans over the driver's seat, trying to see Maggie's unreadable face.

"We have to talk about what happened ..." she begins.

Maggie shrugs. "I was drunk, is all."

"I know ... but I'm worried something's wrong and I don't know what it is ... if it's what happened with Craig ..."

"Nothing happened with Craig," Maggie says flatly.

Iris presses. "You're lying. I can always tell when you're lying!"

"I'm *not* lying," Maggie insists.

Clarissa, Hattie and Rhonda are already headed back carrying white lunch bags printed with bright yellow onions.

165

"Meet me at the pond tonight," Iris begs.

"I can't."

"Maggie, please! Something's wrong and I don't think I can stand it if we don't get it fixed. Will you come?"

Another shrug. "I don't know. I'll try to."

Iris sits back with something like relief. "I'll be there by ten o'clock. Mama and Daddy are usually asleep by then."

~ ~ ~ ~ ~

The clock has just struck eleven in the Deerborne household, and to Iris's vexation, Francie will not go to bed.

When Francie's not drinking away her misery — and she isn't now, thanks to a new bout of fighting with Hank — she's cleaning her misery away.

Last month, when Francie spotted a new wrinkle on her face, every wall got a scrub-down.

When the crop failed a year ago and Hank shut off her clothing allowance, she practically took the color out of the kitchen linoleum.

Tonight, Francie punishes the bathroom because of her newfound "cow fat."

When she couldn't button her skirt this morning, she decided to have a looksee at the scale, and what do you know? She'd gained five pounds. Five whole pounds! For no reason!

She'd eaten the same sausage every day for breakfast, the same BLT for lunch. And now everything was sitting smack on her middle.

As Francie Boraxes the living daylights out of the toilet, Iris sticks her head in the bathroom, carrying a bucket and wearing rubber gloves.

"Mama, I'm really tired," she pleads. "Can I go up to bed now?"

See, when Francie cleans, Iris cleans. That's just the way it works.

"Absolutely not!" Francie exclaims in an elbow-jabbing fury. "I might be your mother, but I am not your slave. You create half the mess in this house, so you're gonna clean up your share!"

Iris decides on action. She steps forward, pretending to reach for the Borax, and sneezes right in Francie's face.

Francie stops mid-scrub. "Iris, what the hell're you thinkin' spreading your germs like that?"

"Sorry, Mama, I think I'm comin' down with somethin'. Which is too bad, 'cuz when I get sick, we all get sick."

"Because you don't know how to keep your germs to yourself!"

"If I get some sleep, I might be able to fight it off."

Francie sighs, "Alright then, go on to bed. God knows I'm used to keepin' this house runnin' all by myself. Why should that change now?"

Iris sets the bucket down and peels off the gloves. "Thank you, Mama. I'll help tomorrow."

"By then it'll all be done," Francie growls.

Iris slips away as Francie lays waste to the bathroom floor. In moments, the child's out the window and gone across the fields like a flash.

Chapter Ten

At half past eleven, Iris breaks through the trees surrounding Sumner Pond, eager to see her friend but there's no Maggie in sight, like she feared. Iris decides to wait until midnight, just in case Maggie's late, too.

There's a chill in the air. Soon, Iris knows, it will be too cold to come to the pond.

Every year, that thought alone grieved her. Each winter, Iris hibernated like the frogs under the ice, locking up her feelings during those long months until the warm water could soothe and strengthen her again.

But tonight, Iris turns her face into the fast-cooling breeze. For the first time, she has no dread of winter. She feels like a second-year sapling, strong enough to stand on its own.

Iris sighs. By the moon's position she can tell it's past midnight. Untangling her cross-legged limbs, Iris stands. As she starts toward the trees, she hears a rustle from that same direction. Relief sweeps through her as Maggie emerges from the brush carrying a bath towel and robe.

"Thank God! I thought I missed you!" Iris calls out.

Maggie stops and frowns at her. "You're still here?"

Her tone stings Iris like an open-handed slap. "What is it? What's wrong?"

But Maggie ignores Iris. Cupping her hands around her mouth, she shouts toward the trees, "Over here, y'all!"

Laughter and yells come from the trees, moving closer. Iris holds her head, unbelieving.

"Maggie, what did you do?"

"It's no big deal," Maggie shrugs.

Suddenly, a crowd of teenagers burst into the clearing, breaking the pond's solitude. Towels, snacks and six-packs of beer fall to the ground.

Clarissa, Rhonda and Hattie tramp towards the shore, followed by Craig Butler, Brian Embrick and Walter Goggins.

Naturally, Clarissa is grumbling. "I don't see why we have to come here." She steps like a tenderfoot on hot coals around the rocks and sawgrass. "This place gives me the heebie jeebies!"

Maggie waves expansively. "'Cuz none of our parents will think to come here! Open your minds and give it a try!"

Craig throws an arm around Maggie's shoulders. He pulls her into his iron frame and kisses her hard on the mouth.

"We already tried it out once," he mumbles into the curve of her neck. "We oughta try it out again."

"Maybe you oughta cool off first." Maggie pulls back, indicating the pond.

"Only if you come with me." Craig shrugs out of his shirt and tosses it aside.

"I'm right behind you." Maggie crouches to pull off her shoes.

Bewildered, Iris kneels next to Maggie, grasping her elbow. "What're you doin'?"

Maggie sets her shoes aside and strips off her socks. "We're havin' a party, Iris. What's it look like?"

Panic rises like bile in Iris's throat as more clothes are shucked and bodies splash into the water.

"This is ours. This is *our* place!"

Iris tries to force Maggie to look her in the eye, but Maggie focuses on unbuttoning her shirt.

"Don't be so stingy," she says.

Iris feels frantic. Crude voices grate in the mild air. Indifferent faces and vulgar bodies desecrate the pond's quiet grace.

"Craig Butler, you better keep your drawers on!" Rhonda cries flirtatiously.

"You afraid it might jump out and bite you?" Craig laughs.

Rhonda screams as Craig unzips his pants and flashes her.

"You put that away, Craig Butler. That's for my eyes only," Maggie laughs. Stripped to her underwear, she heads for the pond.

Desperately, Iris grabs Maggie's arm and spins her around. "Get them out of here," she hisses.

In the background, Hattie shouts to the crowd, "I am not disrobing, if that's what you think."

"We've all seen it about a hundred times, Hattie," Walter Goggins yells back. "I don't see what the big deal is."

"Get them out of here," Iris begs Maggie.

Annoyed, Maggie twists her arm free. "Calm down, Iris. You can't just hog this place!"

Clarissa hollers from the water, "Come on, Maggie, what're you waitin' for?"

That's when Iris sees Brian Embrick peeing into Sumner Pond like it's his personal latrine. This breaks her.

Enraged, she runs at Brian. "Stop that!" she screams, shoving him to the ground. "What is *wrong* with you?! Get out of here!"

"What's your problem, Iris?" Brian laughs. "You of all people know what it's like to need to take a whizz!"

A gaggle of the others overhear and cackle openly.

Iris gapes at one garish face, contorted with laughter, then another. She grips her hands into fists, a madness rising.

"Oh, come on Iris," Brian makes light. "You gotta learn to take a joke."

"Get out of here!" she shrieks. "Get out! Get out! All of you, get out of here! Get out of here, *now!*"

Iris careens into the water, flailing from one intruder to the next, pushing and pulling them toward the shore. Maggie watches vacantly.

"Jesus H. Christ! What's wrong with you?" Craig yells as he wrenches his wrist free of Iris's grasp.

She yanks Rhonda by the hair. "Oh, my God! Iris, that hurts. Let me go! Stop!"

Staggering out of the water, Iris knocks a beer can out of Walter Goggin's hand, snatches his clothes off the ground and shoves them at him.

"Get out of hereeeee!" she screeches.

"She's gone batshit crazy," Clarissa howls from the water.

"Iris, I always knew you smelled bad, but I didn't know you were a nutjob!" laughs Craig.

This drives Iris to the brink. "GET OUT OF MY POND! GET OUT!"

Maggie snaps out of her trance. She approaches Iris and tries to mollify her, whispering, "Iris, calm down."

"GET OUT!"

"Iris. Iris!" Maggie's eyes soften. She holds Iris by the arm, stroking it as she tries to soothe her.

171

Iris turns on Maggie, stung. "What's wrong with you?!" she cries. "You're not like them. You're nothing like them! You lie to them, not me. You lie to them!"

Clarissa materializes from the pond. She stands dripping next to Maggie and Iris, her towel wrapped around her middle, eyes narrowed. "What does she mean by that, Maggie? Did you lie to me?"

"Of course not. I don't know what she's saying," Maggie replies.

Iris frantically gathers up beer cans and chip bags. She shouts at Maggie, "Come on, help me. Help me! What's *wrong* with you??"

Maggie's eyes turn to stone. "*You're* what's wrong with me."

This stops Iris cold, kneeling amidst the trash. She's sober as she looks into Maggie's eyes. "What'd you say?"

"I said, you're what's wrong with me ... Stinky Drawers."

The words hang in the air. The others titter.

"You're lying," Iris says simply.

For a split second, Maggie's mask drops and a flash of sheer pain rends her face. Iris sees it. She stands and approaches Maggie.

"Don't pollute me with your smelly hands," Maggie yells.

Iris swallows hard, letting the pain pass. When she looks back at Maggie, her eyes are kind.

"I don't know what happened to you and I don't care. Because I see you. I know you. And this isn't you."

Iris breaks for the trees and home.

Maggie composes herself. She faces the others and circles her finger around her ear. "That girl is crazy!"

"Come on, Mags," Hattie calls from the pond. "The water's warm."

"We never wanted her anyway," Clarissa says. "We only let her be around us 'cuz she was your pity project."

"Even though we thought it was a mistake," Rhonda adds.

"Still, you gotta admit, Iris is lookin' pretty good these days," Brian Embrick weighs in.

"If she looks so good, why don't you take *her* to prom?" Hattie pouts.

"Oh, come on Hattie. Can't a guy look?"

Craig, dripping from the pond, ropes Maggie around the waist. "Let's see if you float," he teases, pulling her to the water's edge.

"It's too cold," Maggie complains, trying to tug free.

Craig's hands roam over her body as he pulls her wetly to him for a kiss. Suddenly claustrophobic, Maggie struggles. "Craig, not now," she says, backing up. "Wait for later."

"I don't wait." His mouth is on hers, his greedy hands everywhere.

The other boys hoot and cheer Craig on. When Craig shoves a knee between Maggie's legs, something inside her snaps. A white-hot rage starts in her chest and flames from her mouth.

"Get your slimy hands off of me, you disgusting moron!"

Poor, unsuspecting rube, Craig Butler. Before all the world, Maggie knees his family jewels practically through the roof of his mouth, dropping him to the ground like a two-hundred-pound sack of flour.

Craig's tortured shriek causes the other young bucks to moan in sympathy and cover their privates. The girls stand frozen, hands clapped over gaping maws.

Maggie calmly surveys the wreckage of Craig Butler curled into a rocking fetal lump. She wrenches his dime-store ring off her finger and flings it at him.

"If you ever touch me again," she says, "I'll cut your Johnson off with a hacksaw and feed it to your pigs!"

Maggie grabs her shoes, socks and towel from the ground and bolts for the trees.

Clarissa steps in her path. "That's it," she snarls. "You're dead in this town."

Maggie takes in every single staring face. "Considering the town, I'd say that's a victory." Then she's gone like a shot in the dark.

~ ~ ~ ~ ~

The narrator of this tale would like to tell you that Maggie ran after Iris and stopped her. She'd like to report that understandings were met, pain was resolved and a friendship renewed. That two young ladies walked arm-in-arm into WaKeeney High the next day and turned their noses up to those who would revile them. But that's not what happened.

Iris marched home, climbed the maple tree, crawled through her bedroom window and wept until there wasn't an ounce of fluid left in her body.

Then a calm set in, and bone weariness. Iris changed into her pajamas, realized she hadn't wet herself, and knew, with certainty, that she never would again.

Sleep came to Iris with a wave of gratitude for Maggie Richmond. No matter what the future held for them, the

174

bright new girl was the one who cured Iris by showing her what true friendship looked like.

~ ~ ~ ~ ~

On the other end of town, Maggie got into her faithful Packard and flew, like a homing pigeon, to Hazel Atkins's house.

She parked in a copse of trees, where no one could see her car from the road, and, like Iris, wept until she could weep no more.

Then Maggie got out of her car, crossed the gravel drive, Hazel's little patch of lawn, and stood on the dark front porch.

She leaned her forehead against the front door for some time. Then she knocked. Quietly. Insistently.

A light came on above Maggie's head. After a moment, she heard Hazel's voice behind the door. "Who's there?"

"Maggie," she mumbled. "Maggie Richmond."

After a long stretch of nothing, when Maggie was certain the light would snap off again, Hazel opened the door a crack and peered out.

She wore a checked robe and frayed slippers. Her blonde curls fell around her face like an angel's. Her eyes were big as lanterns.

"I'm here to start fresh," Hazel pleaded. "To change."

Maggie didn't move.

"I can't," Hazel said.

"This is who I am," Maggie said. "This is me."

Fresh tears rolled down Maggie's face. Hazel opened the door wide and stepped onto the porch. She wiped Maggie's tears away with the sleeve of her robe. Maggie grasped

Hazel's hand and placed it against her cheek, as Hazel had done before.

Unable to stop, Maggie turned her face and pressed her lips into Hazel's palm.

They stayed this way for an eternity. Then Hazel took Maggie's hand and led her inside, closing the door behind them.

~ ~ ~ ~ ~

As clocks across WaKeeney chime two a.m., Hattie and Rhonda pass a bootlegged cigarette back and forth on the drive home from the debacle at Sumner Pond. But that isn't the current topic. Like Rome, all roads in WaKeeney lead to the prom.

"I don't see why Clarissa gets to decide everything we do before the dance," Hattie complains.

"I thought you liked Stein 'N Steer?" Rhonda says.

"That's not the point! She just decided where we're eating prom night without asking me or my date. I'm just not gonna put up with it anymore!"

Rhonda rolls her eyes, taking a drag from the butt.

"Hattie, you always say you're not gonna put up with it anymore and then you just go ahead and put up with it some more. What's different this time?"

"Maybe I've reached my limit! Maybe I've snapped!"

"What're you gonna do? Tell her off?" Rhonda asks.

"I might!"

"I'd like to see that."

"You think I wouldn't?"

"No. I'd just like to see it, is all," Rhonda replies sincerely.

Hattie pulls up in front of Hazel's house.

"Wait a minute. What're we doing at Hazel's?" Rhonda asks.

"I'm s'posed to pick up some henna for my mom."

"Hattie, you can't do that in the middle of the night!"

"I don't have to bother Hazel," Hattie responds. "She said she'd leave it on the porch and I just remembered."

"Come on Hattie, I'm plum pooped and God forbid my mom finds out I'm not in bed! I'll be grounded for eternity!"

"It'll just be a second. I'll be right back."

Hattie yanks the key from the ignition, hops out and dashes across the street to Hazel's front porch.

Rhonda grouses in the car, then takes the opportunity to retrieve a pair of tweezers and compact from her handbag so she can pluck her eyebrows by starlight.

Hattie scavenges the porch for the package. She looks behind a potted rhododendron, under the love seat swing, inside the mailbox. Nothing.

Stumped, Hattie stands on the porch chewing a fingernail. What the hell. She decides to wake Hazel up. This is an emergency and it's not like Hazel has a husband or kids to attend to in the morning. She can lose five minutes of sleep for her faithful customers.

Rhonda, who now surreptitiously plucks a few copper whiskers that sprout on her chin from time to time, sees Hattie about to knock on Hazel's front door.

"Hattie, what in the Sam Hill are you doing? It's too late to wake her up! It's a good thing Clarissa's not here. You know how she feels about comportment. She'd chap your hide pink with a tongue lashing!"

"I don't happen to give a flying fart at a donut hole what Clarissa would think!" cries Hattie.

The girls glare across the yard at each other, then both break out laughing.

"Hey, maybe Hazel left it on the back porch," Hattie says, still snorting with laughter.

"Can't this wait 'till morning, I'm exhausted!" Rhonda shouts.

"Keep your shirt on! I'll be back inna second!"

Hattie trots around the corner of Hazel's house, disappearing from view as Rhonda groans her annoyance.

Hattie sneaks onto the back porch and rustles around the yard tools and potted plants when she spies a small white package tied with a neat blue ribbon hanging off the back doorknob.

Eureka! Relieved, Hattie walks over and nabs it. As she's retracing her footsteps she hears odd noises coming from Hazel's bedroom window.

Hattie hesitates. It would be spying to go and have a look, but she's undone by curiosity and edges closer to the open window, until her ear is practically resting against the screen.

She hears a woman moan. Holy Toledo! Hattie absolutely cannot resist. She's gotta peek. Then she has a terrible thought. What if it's Len, her very own father in there? God knows her mom complains all the time that he's soft on Hazel.

Now she has to know!

Hattie turns her head slightly and presses her nose right up against the screen, peeking through the open curtains.

~ ~ ~ ~ ~

In the car, Rhonda is done with her tweezing. She's tired, cold and bored. *What the hell is keeping that girl?* Just as Rhonda is about to lay on the horn, she hears Hattie McCoy's blood-curdling scream.

Chapter Eleven

Len McCoy refuses to share a bedroom with his wife, Edith. That's because her snores sound like three alligators fighting in a bathtub every time she takes a breath, and a man's gotta get his rest. But sleep is not on the docket for Len tonight.

A door slams open downstairs, crashing against the wall, followed by his daughter Hattie's hysterical sobs. The sobbing racket then stomps up the stairs and bursts into Edith's room across the hall.

At first, Len does nothing. Edith's been handling Hurricane Hattie since puberty and that gives Len permission to pull an extra pillow over his head. Then Edith brays his name.

Len sighs and rolls out of bed. He pads to his wife's room to find Hattie collapsed in her mother's arms.

"What in tarnation's goin' on in here?" Len yells. "This better be important, Hattie, if you're gonna create a commotion when every sensible human being should be asleep!"

Edith looks up at him, righteous with anger.

"Oh, I think you're gonna take a great deal of interest in what Hattie has to tell you, Len McCoy," she says. "I think you're gonna find it *very* interesting indeed!"

Len crosses his arms. "Well, what the hell is it?"

Hattie raises her tear-stained face and tries to get the horrible words out of her mouth. "It's Maggie ... and Hazel!"

"You mean Hazel Atkins?" Len asks, a sudden concern in his eyes.

"Yes, your cute-as-a-button Hazel," Edith spits. "She is *not* what she seems to be. Not one tiny whit." She turns to her daughter. "You tell him, Hattie. Tell him what Hazel did!"

"I saw them! Maggie and Hazel!" she gasps. "It was awful. I saw them ... together!"

~ ~ ~ ~ ~

It takes just twenty minutes for Len to gather up two trucks, eight men, two baseball bats, some rocks and a shovel.

All of this rolls up Hazel's gravel drive, followed by the men grimly exiting the trucks.

Len and Earl Hoover carry the baseball bats. Gary Beaumont has the shovel. Len's brother, Norm, wears thick leather gardener's gloves. Three farmhands and WaKeeney's own Sheriff's Deputy, Harold Diebold, carry the rest.

Len reaches Hazel's Studebaker first. He winds up and caves in the rear window. The crash sets off a wordless frenzy.

Norm McCoy punches in Hazel's house windows with his leather fists.

Earl Hoover's bat takes out the passenger windows of Hazel's car.

Gary Beaumont smashes the windows of the hair salon with his shovel, while the other men trash the house façade.

They pull down decorative molding, yank up plants, rip down the hanging loveseat.

No one hears the soft click of Hazel unlocking her front door. Nor do they register the door opening, or witness

181

Hazel stepping gingerly onto her front porch, swallowing terror.

She's dressed herself with impeccable care. Tan kid heels. A tweed pencil skirt. A stiff white blouse. A reproachless cloche hat. Her best mahogany leather handbag hangs on one shoulder and an overnight suitcase is gripped in the other hand. She clutches car keys in her fist.

One by one the men become aware of Hazel as she walks down her front steps.

All destruction stops. The men, breathing heavy, their blood up, stare at their target as if they could bury her with their eyes.

Trembling, Hazel comes down the last three steps and carefully weaves her way through the frozen throng. She briefly looks sidewise, seeking some kind of protection from the Sheriff's Deputy, but Diebold won't meet her eye.

Girding herself, Hazel navigates around broken shards of glass and uprooted plants toward her car. The men move as one, circling her.

Len McCoy looks her up and down, hands twitching on the bat.

"I guess men like me aren't good enough for you, are they, bitch?" he spits. Then he reaches out and rips the cloche hat off Hazel's head, crushing it in his hands.

Hazel cries out. It takes a moment to master herself. She smooths her disheveled hair, fighting to maintain her dignity. She takes a shaky breath, then continues stepping carefully around the front of her car until she reaches the driver's side door.

She wrenches it open, gasping as glass shards rain down her leg, then shoves her suitcase and shoulder bag across the bench seat.

She slides into the bashed-up vehicle, slamming the door shut, fumbling a key into the ignition. That's when — *Crack!* — one of the farm hands spider-webs Hazel's windshield with a hammer.

She will not scream. She won't.

With shaking hands she turns the key, sparking the engine to life. She puts the car in reverse, her hands bloodless on the steering wheel.

The men part as she backs through them, coming to stand at the side of the road as Hazel puts the gear in drive. Len looms in front of Hazel's car, as if daring her to run him down. The engine idles.

After a moment, he approaches the shattered driver's side window, leans down and looks at Hazel with contempt. She keeps her eyes front, waiting.

"We just gave you back your sorry life," he grunts. "It won't happen again."

Hazel presses her foot to the gas pedal. Her car leaps forward, spitting gravel.

It isn't until every last man disappears from her rear-view mirror that Hazel allows great racking sobs to escape her body.

~ ~ ~ ~ ~

As Hazel weaves her battered car into the inky black night, Maggie lays curled in the fetal position on her living room floor.

183

Gerald stands over her, a belt clenched tightly in his right fist. Grace has wedged herself between them, her manicured hands pressed against his chest.

Emmett sits at the base of the stairs, his thumb in his mouth, a toddler again. Tallulah hovers on the step above, clutching her stuffed dog, Charlie, to her chest.

"We can go back to that doctor in Saint Louis," Grace pleads with Gerald. "He said he could help ... they help lots of kids like this ... help them be normal."

Maggie's face is mottled and red. There are ridged marks on her arms from Gerald's belt lashes. His craggy face is riven with grief as he slumps on the couch, his face buried in his hands.

"What's wrong with Daddy?" Tallulah cries out.

"Shut up, Lula!" Emmet shouts. "Just shut up!"

"It's okay, babies," Grace says, moving to the stairs. "It's okay."

She leans down and holds Emmett, her hand grasping for Tallulah, who inches carefully down into her mother's arms.

Maggie looks through the curtain of hair that's fallen over her face to see Gerald weeping. This is worse, so much worse than the belt. She crawls to him, kneels in front of him.

"Don't cry, Daddy. Please, don't cry."

Gerald places his hands on his daughter's hair, stroking it. "You were my beautiful baby. Such a precious child. You woke up every morning smiling. Happy to see us, to see the world."

"I'm sorry, Daddy," Maggie says dully.

"We did something wrong ... *I* did something wrong."

"You didn't do anything wrong."

"You came so perfect, straight from heaven ..."

"You didn't do anything, Daddy. It's me, I did it." Maggie's numb voice rides a thin thread of determination. "I'll fix it. You'll see. It'll be better. Don't worry. I'll make it all better."

Maggie kisses her father's hands and gets to her feet. She walks to the front door, turns and looks back at her family. "I love you," she says. Then she's gone once more into the night.

The Richmond family stays as they are for some time, a tableau of confusion and pain, until a horrible premonition overtakes Grace.

She abandons Emmet and Tallulah on the stairs, racing to the front door.

She throws it open and screams her first child's name into the night over and over, until her throat can't scream anymore.

~ ~ ~ ~ ~

It's as if Grace Richmond's cries cross the prairie and wake Iris from a fitful sleep. She bolts up in bed, echoing Maggie's name, then realizes she hears actual voices coming up from the kitchen below.

Iris throws on a robe and her glasses. She rushes downstairs and bursts into the kitchen to find Francie, Edith and Hattie loudly talking, their words laced with malice and pleasure. Hank sits at the kitchen table nursing a whiskey.

Francie wheels on Iris, "I knew it!" she snaps. "Even though I never met her in the flesh, from everything I heard I just *knew* there was something wrong about that girl!"

Iris catches her breath. "What's happened, Mama?"

"You, behaving like an idiot," Francie spits. "That's what happened. Now we're gonna be the town gossip, you bein' friends with that perverted girl."

"Francie, there ain't no cause to take it out on Iris!" Hank shouts.

"What is it? What happened?" Iris begs.

"Hattie found Maggie and Hazel together," Edith informs Iris, scandalized glee in her voice.

Hattie takes this cue, handily crying afresh. She's born to the role of the injured party here, having had her eyeballs scathed by iniquity.

"Hazel cuts Maggie's hair," Iris offers, confused.

"Not like that, Iris," Francie snipes, only too happy to set her straight. "They were together ..." she waves her cigarette. "I can't even say how!"

"Lying down on the bed. Being immoral," Edith supplies, reaching over to hug Hattie close. "My poor girl is traumatized for life. The news is all over town. The boys have already been over to Hazel's and run her off."

Panicked, Iris grabs Hattie's arm, "Where's Maggie?"

"Owww, Iris, that hurts!" Hattie whines.

"Don't you touch my daughter, Iris!" Edith growls.

But Iris is like a spaniel after a bird. She shakes Hattie. "Where is she?" she demands. "Tell me, now!"

Hattie looks up from her mother's arms, a glint of gossipy delight shining through her tears.

"Some of the gang were still at Sumner Pond and saw Maggie come back after she'd lit out of there earlier," Hattie says. "They saw her walk right into the pond 'til the water covered her head. Just like Charlotte Owings. They said she killed herself, I guess 'cuz she's a deviant."

Whack! Iris slaps Hattie square in the face with all her might, leaving a gratifying red hand print on her cheek.

"How dare you hit my child!" Edith brays. "I swear Francie, if she weren't your daughter I'd run her through with a skewer!"

Hank bolts out of his chair, looming over the McCoy women. "I think it's high time you two clear out of this house! Right now!"

Edith shoots Hank an indignant look and peels a sobbing Hattie off the chair to leave. Hank kicks the door shut behind them.

"Iris! Where on God's green earth do you think you're going?" Francie yells as she watches Iris pull on her boots. "Don't you even *think* of stepping outside this house!"

But Iris is up and out the door before Francie can move.

~ ~ ~ ~ ~

Dawn's light is just breaking over Sumner Pond, but damn-near half the town of WaKeeney is on her shores. Once Edith knew about the "lesbian activity" at Hazel's, every phone rang off its hook. And everybody had to come for a looksee.

Sheriff Breeland and his deputies, Marcus Cole and Harold Diebold — back from his dirty work at Hazel's house — command the scene. A crew of men on a skiff drag the pond for Maggie's body.

Iris arrives sweating and breathless. She's spotted by a frantic woman who runs to her. "Are you Iris?" the woman asks. "Iris Deerborne?"

187

It's Grace Richmond, eyes wild, unpinned hair falling free into her bare face. Iris nods, concerned. "I am."

"I hoped it was you. I'm Maggie's mother, Grace. She told me you were her friend."

"I *am* her friend."

Grace desperately clutches at Iris's sleeve. "Have you seen my Maggie?"

"Not since last night. Around midnight?"

Grace cocks her head as if listening for the sound of her daughter's voice. "I don't know where she is," she mumbles. "I drove all over town, but I didn't see her."

Iris comforts her. "I'm sure Maggie's all right. She's a strong girl who can take care of herself."

Grace takes a breath. "I hope you're right. I hope you're right. But, if you see her ... will you tell her to come home?"

"I will."

Grace looks Iris full in the face with beseeching eyes. "You're her friend, aren't you?"

"Yes, I'm her friend."

"Tell her it doesn't matter ..." Grace says. "Tell her I don't care anymore ... I don't care if she was bad."

"But, Mrs. Richmond," Iris says with truth. "Maggie was never bad."

As if dropping a heavy load, Grace sinks a bit. She looks at Iris, clear-eyed. "No, she wasn't. Was she?" Grace pushes the hair out of her face and takes Iris's hand. "You just tell her to come home ... tell her that her mama loves her! Tell her to come home."

Suddenly, Deputy Cole shouts out from the skiff, "We got something!"

Grace lurches away from Iris, pulled to the edge of the pond as if on a string.

Iris closes her eyes, not wanting to see what Deputy Cole's got on the end of his pole. She looks up at the sky, the stars fading away as the morning sun comes on. She sees one last shooting star fall from the heavens.

Her eyes close gently. *I wish I may, I wish I might, have the wish I wish tonight. Let her disappear. Let her disappear. Let her disappear.*

Deputy Cole pulls up the heavy object snagged on the end of his pole.

"Is it the body?" Sheriff Breeland shouts.

"I don't know, I can't quite make it out."

"Harold, shine the lantern on 'im!"

Deputy Diebold shines a flashlight at the object on the end of the pole. As one, all eyes strain to make it out.

Francie, just arrived, stands next to Iris. "What the hell is that?" Francie asks. Her eyes narrow into a suspicious slits. "Why, that looks like ..."

Not a body. A dress. The mud-laden, algae-ridden corpse of Francie's hideous pink prom abomination!

The crowd exhales. Grace falls weeping to her knees. And Iris laughs with relief.

"Iris Mabel Deerborne! Do you know how much time and labor I put into that dress? It is *not* funny!" Francie scolds.

Iris can't stop laughing. "I know Mama, I never did have no sense of humor. None whatsoever."

~ ~ ~ ~ ~

Weeks pass. Gossip surrounding the "tragic new girl" fades as prom talk resumes. Who's taking who. Where they're supping beforehand. Where they'll park after.

The day before the big event, Iris applies her Woolworth's makeup in front of her vanity mirror as she gets ready for school. When she's finished, she places a new, sleek pair of eyeglasses on her nose — a gift from her daddy.

Things have changed in the Deerborne household. The day after Maggie's disappearance, Iris heard her father cleaning out the freshly restocked living room bar, tossing every bottle while ignoring Francie's vehement and prolonged protestations.

After dinner, days later, when Francie cornered Hank and complained about Iris's new glasses and how they couldn't afford such extravagances, Hank told Francie, in no uncertain terms, that unless she could be kind to their daughter, one of them would be moving out. And it wouldn't be Iris.

"We lost one beautiful girl. A girl who loved our daughter," Hank said, his voice breaking, "And I'll be damned if we lose another. Not on my watch."

Since that night, Francie's been cleaning like a woman possessed. But she hasn't touched a drop of liquor.

~ ~ ~ ~ ~

Prom morning, Iris walks onto campus wearing a new ivory twinset and bell-skirt she bought with her egg money. Her dark, thick hair is tucked up into a sleek twist she learned to do from one of Francie's *Sears* magazines, and she wears a light pink lipstick that is excellent for "selling lips."

There are other marked differences in Iris. She wears her shoulders thrown back, her head held high, her spine straight, and she smiles often without knowing it. She also has a touch of Maggie's fire behind her eyes.

When Hattie and Rhonda sashay past Iris at her locker, whispering and nudging, Iris could give a rat's ass.

~ ~ ~ ~ ~

In chemistry lab, Clarissa boycotts partnering with Iris by sitting on a stool, filing her red-tipped fingernails, leaving Iris to man the station as she sees fit.

"Clarissa, why're you sittin' there letting Iris do all the work?" Miss Steingarten bellows. "You're already on my stink list and believe me you, you're not gonna want to be there over winter break or you'll *have* no winter break!"

Iris wordlessly hands Clarissa a pair of crucible tongs. Sighing, Clarissa takes them.

~ ~ ~ ~ ~

At lunch time, Iris carries her food tray past a gaggle of gossiping Songbirds in the cafeteria and a throng of football players arm-wrestling on an outdoor table.

She arrives at a birch tree on the margin of campus where Sally Fuller eats a homemade tuna fish sandwich.

Word is, Sally's parents recently divorced, which is, as yet, unheard of in Trego County. Worse, her daddy left town with a married woman and never looked back.

The stress of it all gave Sally a painful, unsightly case of the shingles. The sores, hot and red, snake across the lower portion of Sally's face, marking her as WaKeeney's latest Untouchable.

Rather than take advantage of her reprieve, Iris rushed to Sally's side, like a volunteer fire brigade, to douse the twin flames of shame and isolation.

Since then, she and the other social misfits have found lunchtime solace under the birch trees. Occasionally, tides of their laughter will lap across campus, right up to the Songbirds table.

~ ~ ~ ~ ~

This afternoon, Iris walks Old Junction Road after school by herself, as she did in the beginning of this story. She's halfway home when she hears the familiar roar of a '55 Ford pick-up coming up behind her, blasting "Ally Oop" by the Hollywood Argyles.

The truck pulls even with Iris. Pacing her.

Hal Beacham's at the wheel this time. Mike Whittaker rides shotgun. Derry isn't with them, which makes matters worse, since he's the only one who might've tried to talk his brother out of torturing Iris.

"Hey, Stinky Drawers," Hal calls out. "Long time no see."

Iris chooses not to respond.

"That's 'cuz she was catchin' rides from a dyke," Mike sneers. "Never knew you liked girls, Iris. What'd you and your dead lesbo friend do together?"

"I bet you let *her* feel your melons," Hal laughs.

"If you let some damn lesbo at 'em," Mike leers, "you're sure as hell gonna let me at 'em."

The small hairs on the back of Iris's neck stand up. Pinpricks of cold sweat pop out on her upper lip.

"Don't you make me get out of this truck, Stinky," Mike warns. "If I gotta get outa this truck, I'm gonna touch a lot more than them melons."

Hal opens the driver's door. "C'mon Iris, get in. We got a place for you right between us."

"Don't make me come get you," taunts Mike.

Without breaking stride, Iris veers off the shoulder of the road into the bordering field. She slams her books on the ground and snatches up a rock.

"Don't you even think about it, Iris!" Mike threatens.

"Oh, I'm done thinkin'," Iris shouts.

And following the technique from the Bud Daley/Maggie Richmond playbook, Iris points her free hand to where she wants the rock to go, then fires it off, smashing in Hal's nose.

"Jesus H. Christ, she hit me! That bitch hit me!" Hal's nose gushes a delightful river of red.

Iris grabs more rocks off the ground and hurtles them with ferocity at the truck.

Smash! Crash! Bash! Half the rocks hit pay dirt, cracking the passenger window, denting the door, bouncing off the windshield.

"Don't you ever touch me!" Iris shouts in cold fury. "Don't you ever touch me again, you bastards! I'll kill you! *I'll kill you!*"

"Let's get the hell outta here!" Mike yells.

Hal doesn't need to be told twice. He slams the door shut, puts the gas pedal to the floorboards and spits blood out as he yells, "Crazy dyke!"

Smash! One large rock cracks the rear window. "COW FUCKERS!" Iris screams. She chases after them, rage making her mighty.

In moments, the truck is a shrinking, battered reflection in Iris's triumphant eyes.

~ ~ ~ ~ ~

In the Deerborne kitchen, late that afternoon, Francie and Edith play a hand of Canasta over coffee and cigarettes.

The booze may be out, but if Hank expects Francie to give up the nicotine, too, he's got another thing coming.

Quietly, Iris appears in the doorway, wearing the champagne satin prom dress she'd tried on for Maggie in Lula Mae's Bridal and Dance Shop weeks ago. She looks a picture.

Deep in gossipy conjecture, Francie and Edith don't notice Iris at first.

"They still haven't found that girl's body," Edith gossips. "I can garun-damn-tee you it's rotting away down there right next to Charlotte Owings in one of them underground caves."

Iris steps into view. "I don't believe a girl who could throw rocks like Maggie Richmond would let herself die of shame," she interrupts.

Both women lay eyes on Iris. A surprised quiet greets her calm poise.

"I believe she walked out the other side of that pond," Iris says, "hopped a freight train and snubbed her nose at all the petty, small-minded people who couldn't see her shine."

Francie huffs, deciding to change the subject. "Where in God's name are you goin' dressed like that?" she asks Iris.

"Maybe she's goin' to prom after all," Edith says.

"I wouldn't go to that prom to save my life," Iris smiles. "I've got a date."

"With who?" Francie asks, disbelieving.

"A boy, Mama."

"What boy? There ain't no boy."

Iris steps forward, forcing Francie's gaze to hers. "I'll never be as beautiful as you are, Mama," she says. "But I've got a date with a boy tonight and I hope you can be happy for me."

Before Francie can sputter a response, Iris leans down and puts her arms around her mother in a warm embrace.

"I do love you, Mama," she whispers.

Iris holds on a moment longer. Then lets her mama go and strides out the back door, leaving Francie and Edith sitting at the kitchen table with cigarettes burning down between their fingers.

Chapter Twelve

Iris stands at the edge of Sumner Pond. The breeze lifts her skirt like a champagne cloud. She shades her eyes with her hand, watching an orangey-pink sun hover over the water.

After a moment, my Jeff emerges from the trees. He's wearing a rented tux in an unnatural powder blue. His cowlicks have never been wilder. And his shirt's partially untucked.

"You're late," Iris teases.

Jeff grins. "There was somethin' I had to get." He holds out a delicate corsage of the flowers that are Iris's namesake.

"They're beautiful," she says.

Jeff places the corsage on her neckline, fumbling with a pin. "I don't wanna stab you," he apologizes.

"You won't."

The pin's a chore. "Birthing a calf is easier than gettin' this thing on!" he sighs.

"I believe in you, Jeff Owings," Iris encourages.

Finally, the corsage sticks. It's lopsided, but lovely. Iris takes Jeff's hands and looks a concerned question into his eyes. "Is this all right? You bein' here?" she asks.

Jeff looks out over my resting place. He means it when he says, "It is now."

Then he holds out his hand. "Would you like to dance?"

Iris takes a deep breath and accepts that hand. Soon their dancing forms become water-borne bodies, Iris in a chemise, Jeff in his undershirt.

Iris leans her head back in the constant waters of Sumner Pond as Jeff rolls to his feet. He takes her hand and pulls her through the water, carving languid figure eights with her body. Then he pulls Iris toward him until she floats into his arms. He leans down and kisses her.

I fade as they bloom.

The last thing I see is a peculiar panorama of the sky. That vast blanket of firmament distorted. Its red-purple early evening hues bleed sharply into the curvature of the earth, as if captured in a prism.

Limited. Enclosed.

This is the view through Iris's eyeglasses that sit atop her satin dress, folded neatly on the shore.

Then slowly the lenses shift and the world comes into focus. I can see the beauty of the sky through Iris's glasses as she would see it. Perfectly clear.

THE END

Acknowledgments & About The Author

Back in the '90s, when I was still a struggling "Wacktress" (waiter/actress) I'd begun dabbling in playwriting as acting parts weren't exactly rolling in.

My now-friend, Peter Fox (it's all because of you Pierre, as I'm sure you know) produced and directed my first one-act play, *But That Wasn't Sex,* at the Alliance Repertory Theater in Burbank.

Despite having a nightmare before the premiere of the entire play performed in German on a train platform in Gstaad instead of Bronx-ese in a women's toilet, I was overjoyed by the actual production.

(Joel Stoffer you will always be my Edward Norton.)

Two more one-acts — *The Lion Sleeps Tonight* and *The Bridge* — under Peter's helm followed, then he asked if I'd like to write one-third of a film triptych set on a farm with him and playwright/screenwriter Garry Williams.

The goal was to make a low-budget film that told the story of youth, middle-age and old-age amidst hay and heifers.

"Why a farm?" you might ask. Peter had a friend who offered his farm as a free location.

I was intrigued by the chance to write the "youth" segment, as my grandma Ellen was born on a farm in WaKeeney, Kansas in 1914, and I believe it shaped her into the nurturing, empathetic, grounded woman who was my angel on earth, so I set to work.

While the farm movie never materialized, it was the

catalyst for the birth of Iris Deerborne and Maggie Richmond and for that, Peter, I am eternally grateful.

To The Stars (then *Loving Iris*) was expanded from a thirty-minute script into a feature-length screenplay while I attended the UCLA Master's Program in screenwriting under the tutelage of former professor Hal Ackerman.

It cannot be overstated how much influence Hal had in helping me turn what was basically an unstructured, monologue-infested stew into a three-act screenplay with set-up, conflict and resolution.

My first literary agents, Ann Blanchard and Cori Wellins, gave me the confidence to believe that a film set in the 1961 Bible-Belt, boasting a protagonist who wears diapers, was viable.

My current agents, Lee Keele, Amanda Smith, Bayard Maybank and Bob Hohman at Gersh, continue to fan the flames of my passion for screenwriting.

Lee and Amanda, in particular, help make everything I attempt better with their insightful notes, even in the face of my petulance.

One thing is certain, *To The Stars* would never have become a novel if it weren't for all the folks involved in making the film.

It was their excellent cinematic work that inspired me to re-commit to the novel adaptation and even catalyzed new voices and deeper character work.

I'm indebted to producers Kristin Mann and Laura D. Smith of *Prowess Pictures* who fought tooth and nail to find financing, manage the physical and post-production of the film, execute its festivals run, sales and distribution.

Director Martha Stephens made my film experience a

dream. She worked with me as if I were a playwright when it came to any changes needed in the script for production, which is to say, she consulted with me throughout production and was respectful of the source material.

When I finally sat down to watch Martha's film on my computer on a Tuesday at 3 a.m., bolstered by a tumbler of Absolut, I couldn't believe my eyes — nor my luck!

The film was shot in delicious black-and-white that instantly transported me to a time and place reminiscent of Bogdanovich's *The Last Picture Show* or *Paper Moon*.

There was absolutely nothing anachronistic in the film as Martha is a stickler for detail and veracity.

The screenplay was initially set in WaKeeney, Kansas, (like the novel is now) but when it became clear we were going to shoot in Enid, Oklahoma, the script had to change to reflect that. In Martha's world there is no cheating one location for another.

Finally, Martha's collaboration with the actors rendered specific, moving, high-caliber performance across the board.

Seeing the gorgeous film she created was certainly enough to make me love her forever, but I now value her even more passionately as a dear friend.

The film's actors also galvanized my imagination for the adaptation with their remarkable performances.

Thanks to Kara Hayward for bringing Iris Deerborne to life with intelligence, tenderness, playfulness and love. Your performance is indelible.

To Liana Liberato, much was asked of you in the role of Maggie Richmond, ranging from confidence, to fierce protectiveness, to raw vulnerability and you knocked it out of the park. I believe the word flung around during post-production to describe you as Maggie was "incandescent."

My gratitude to Jordana Spiro is boundless. With just two days' notice she was flown from L.A. to Oklahoma to portray stone-cold bitch, Francie Deerborne.

Somehow Jordana managed to imbue a fairly one-note character with pathos, relatability and unexpected humor.

Jordana's performance inspired a much deeper dive into Francie's character in this novel.

Malin Akerman's Grace Richmond was flawless. From the moment she stepped on-screen we could see that beneath Grace's polished exterior lay a deeply insecure, frightened woman at a loss as to how to heal her family.

Tony Hale's Gerald Richmond was a complete departure from the comedic roles Tony's best known for, yet his final scene as the Richmond patriarch demonstrates his incredible range as an actor.

I was surprised when Shea Whigham accepted the fairly small role of Hank Deerborne, given his ocean of A-list credits. But Shea didn't phone in one second.

When he walks onscreen Shea brings Hank's entire history with him. With just a look, or a movement, we can feel the weight of a troubled marriage and his addiction to it resting heavy on Hank's shoulders. It's testament to Shea's craft as one of the finest actors of our time.

Adelaide Clemens' performance as Hazel Atkins is a stunner. Again, brought on with very short notice, Adelaide channeled Hazel from some inexplicable source.

She perfectly captured Hazel's deep pain of repressing her true self to survive the claustrophobic community she lives in, while longing is always just a look or a breath away.

More beautifully still, is how Adelaide captured Hazel's

dignity when confronted by a shaming, dangerous mob.

Lucas Jade Zumann is a gem playing Jeff Spencer, the high school lone-wolf slash dreamboat.

Lucas brings incredible empathy and vulnerability to the role, not to mention a heap-load of charisma.

Rounding out the cast, elegant Madisen Beaty (as Clarissa Dell), hilarious Sophi Bairley (as Hattie McCoy) and scene-stealing Lauren Stephenson (as Rhonda Robertson), made being mean girls look like a lot of fun.

I owe my greatest debt of gratitude for this novel to my deft, determined, creative editor Diane Cyr.

Diane's assiduous eye for detail, her painstaking assessment of prose and her dogged determination to force my best work out of me have elevated this final draft to heights I could never have reached alone. Thank you, my talented colleague and friend!

Then there's Jeannine Chanin-Penn. A visionary artist who has kindly leapt in to create two of my book covers and most of the artwork on my blogs and social media.

Jeannine's *To The Stars* cover perfectly captures the private parts of Iris's world that are her own kind of *Secret Garden*. Thank you, my lovely J.

Now I have the opportunity to thank my family. My daughters Rowan and Willa, who are creatives in their own right, inspire me daily.

My girls. You've made me a better writer and human because you've both challenged me to explore new perspectives and listen to voices other than my own. Especially when I didn't want to.

Because of you, I've turned full-on sci-fi geek, binging any and every *Star Wars* iteration — even the bad ones we've watched twice. The entire *Harry Potter* book and film series. *The Mandalorian* — I mean, Baby Yoda. *Avatar the Last Airbender* — the Sky Bison!

I do think, however, you've joined my passion for anything Wes Anderson, Coen Brothers, Alfonso Cuaron and Quentin Tarantino — though I really think we're in need of a Sofia Coppola weekend.

At the same time you've introduced me to Andrea Arnold, Alma Har'el, Sean Baker, Roger Eggers, Ari Aster, Bong Joon-ho — but we *do* need more women. I hope you plan to change that!

Your social activism inspired me to read *White Fragility*, to watch *The Social Dilemma*, to be catalyzed toward fighting against climate change and all the good things that truly matter.

I am so proud of the young women you've become and I look forward to continuing to learn from you both throughout my life. Having the honor of being your mother has brought me a joy that's impossible to express in words.

Finally, I'm thrilled to thank my greatest hero and champion, my husband Michael Colleary.

Though I tease you about not liking *To The Stars* the script, we both know that every piece of writing I've produced has been influenced and improved by you.

Your deep wisdom about story, structure, mise en scene, concept and character pales in comparison to the wisdom you have about what it means to be a successful writer.

Because of you I've learned to never overly-fetishize any one piece of material which allows me to keep creating new work and continue developing my craft.

When I've felt put-upon or outraged by studio notes,

you've taught me to look beneath the surface to find the "spirit of the note" in order to find my own creative solutions while remaining a team player.

Basically, you've taught me to get over myself and frankly, that's the most powerful tool for productivity.

I am also grateful for the husband and father you are. I'm so lucky to bask in the glow of your deep, kind, kind heart.

Without your support so many posts, books and scripts would still be sitting on a shelf in my brain.

I love you. I love you. Amen.

Dear Reader – If you enjoyed reading *To The Stars* it would mean the world if you would leave a review on Amazon. Xxx S